K19 SECURITY SOLUTIONS
TEAM ONE
—BOOK THREE—

MISTLETOE'S MAGIC

USA TODAY BESTSELLING AUTHOR

HEATHER SLADE

MISTLETOE'S MAGIC
© 2018 Heather Slade

This book is a work of fiction. The names, characters, places and incidents are products of the writer's imagination or have been used fictitiously and are not to be construed as real. Any resemblance to persons, living or dead, actual events, locale or organizations is entirely coincidental.

Paperback:
979-8-88649-116-6

MORE FROM AUTHOR HEATHER SLADE

BUTLER RANCH

Kade's Worth
Brodie's Promise
Maddox's Truce
Naughton's Secret
Mercer's Vow
Kade's Return
Butler Ranch Christmas

WICKED WINEMAKERS
FIRST LABEL

Brix's Bid
Ridge's Release
Press' Passion
Zin's Sins
Tryst's Temptation

WICKED WINEMAKERS
SECOND LABEL

Beau's Beloved
Coming Soon:
Cru's Crush
Bones' Bliss
Snapper's Seduction
Kick's Kiss

ROARING FORK RANCH

Coming Soon:
Roaring Fork Wrangler
Roaring Fork Roughstock
Roaring Fork Rockstar
Roaring Fork Rooker
Roaring Fork Bridger

THE ROYAL AGENTS
OF MI6

Make Me Shiver
Drive Me Wilder
Feel My Pinch
Chase My Shadow
Find My Angel

K19 SECURITY
SOLUTIONS TEAM ONE

Razor's Edge
Gunner's Redemption
Mistletoe's Magic
Mantis' Desire
Dutch's Salvation

K19 SECURITY
SOLUTIONS TEAM TWO

Striker's Choice
Monk's Fire
Halo's Oath
Tackle's Honor
Onyx's Awakening

K19 SHADOW OPERATIONS
TEAM ONE

Code Name: Ranger
Code Name: Diesel
Code Name: Wasp
Code Name: Cowboy
Code Name: Mayhem

K19 ALLIED INTELLIGENCE
TEAM ONE

Code Name: Ares
Code Name: Cayman
Code Name: Poseidon
Code Name: Zeppelin
Code Name: Magnet

K19 ALLIED INTELLIGENCE
TEAM TWO

Coming Soon:
Code Name: Puck
Code Name: Michelangelo
Code Name: Typhon
Code Name: Hornet
Code Name: Reaper

PROTECTORS
UNDERCOVER

Undercover Agent
Undercover Emissary
Coming Soon:
Undercover Savior
Undercover Infidel
Undercover Assassin

THE INVINCIBLES
TEAM ONE

Decked
Edged
Grinded
Riled
Smoked

THE INVINCIBLES
TEAM TWO

Bucked
Irished
Sainted
Hammered
Ripped

THE UNSTOPPABLES
TEAM ONE

Furied
Merried

COWBOYS OF
CRESTED BUTTE

A Cowboy Falls
A Cowboy's Dance
A Cowboy's Kiss
A Cowboy Stays
A Cowboy Wins

Table of Contents

1

Mantis, Alegria, and Dutch

—Mantis—

Compared to some of the places I'd been forced to sleep during my career, the hospital recliner was damn comfortable.

I shifted to my left side, hoping it would relieve some of the pressure on the right, where a bullet had struck my hip, requiring pelvic reconstruction surgery. The good news was, it hadn't been life threatening and none of my organs had been compromised. The arthritic pain, however, was unrelenting.

I looked over at the woman lying in the hospital bed, hoping her injuries wouldn't result in a similar life of pain. No one deserved to live with the kind I had to, but Alegria deserved it less than anyone I'd ever known.

We'd met at the United States Air Force Academy when I was a senior and she was an international student one year behind me. I remembered the day our Air Officer Commanding, AOC, introduced Manon

"Alegria" Mondreau to the squadron. She was the most beautiful woman I'd ever seen. Still was.

Her ebony-black hair was pulled back into the tight bun required by Air Force regulations, highlighting her mesmerizing, almond-shaped, gray-blue eyes.

How many times had I kissed her pouty, cherry-colored lips and ran my hands over her seductively sculpted nubile body? Hundreds.

"Any change?" asked Dutch, who'd known both Manon and me since those early days when we were all cadets, anxious to begin pilot training and get on with our careers.

I shook my head. "Nothing."

"Why don't you take a break? I can sit with her for the next couple of hours."

"Thanks, but I'll stick around."

"Mantis—"

I raised my hand. "I have to be here, Dutch. Don't fight me on this."

My friend nodded and sat in one of the other recliners the hospital staff had agreed to bring into the room.

"She's out of intensive care. That's a good sign, right?" Dutch asked.

It was, but they still had no idea whether the damage to Manon's spinal cord would have lasting effects.

"What happened between you two? Last I heard, you were thinking about proposing."

As Dutch well knew, I'd taken an assignment. One she didn't want me to.

***

"You volunteer more than anyone else. Why?"

"It's my duty, Manon. It's what I signed up for."

"It's no longer a duty. You retired. We agreed—"

"No. Stop right there. We didn't agree to anything. You demanded I quit, and I refused. That's the way it went down."

She shook her head and stormed off. There'd been a time I would've gone after her, but no more. She'd spent just as much time stateside as she had in France, yet she still lived by her native country's work ethic. Or lack of it.

It wasn't that she didn't like to work; Manon was just able to compartmentalize better than I was. She could say no to assignments without thinking twice. I couldn't remember ever turning one down.

A few minutes later, she was back. "If you go, we're finished."

"I won't choose you over my country, Manon."

***

What had made matters worse, the assignment required me to go deep undercover, and during that time, no one knew whether I was dead or alive, and if I was still breathing, when I might resurface.

I had come back, finally, but Manon was steadfast in her refusal to forgive me for what she considered a betrayal.

I tried to get in touch with her when I first returned, but she'd refused to answer my calls. I knew from Doc that she was still on the K19 team, but the boss hadn't encouraged me to continue pursuing her.

"Hold back for now," he'd advised. "She knows you're back. Let her come to you."

I'd questioned Doc's advice, but in the end, abided by it. What choice did I have? She refused to respond to my calls, texts, or emails.

"Is she with someone else?" I'd asked.

"Not that I'm aware of. However, Mantis, the personal lives of K19 team members are none of my business."

I almost laughed at Doc's proclamation, given the man had his nose in everyone else's business about as much as my best friend, Dutch, did.

I stood and walked over to the bed when Manon groaned. I stroked her forehead, willing her to open her eyes and look at me.

"*Mon coeur,*" I whispered when she did.

"*Où suis-je?*"

"*L'hôpital.*" I was reaching the limit of words I knew in French, besides the obvious ones everyone knew. "You were shot."

"Petrov?"

I nodded.

"Surgery?"

"Yes."

She turned her head and looked away from me, noticing for the first time that Dutch was in the room. She reached out her hand for him in the way I would've expected her to reach for me.

I met Dutch's eyes when he stood, and in them, I saw sadness and guilt.

The man who'd been my best friend for twenty years took his time walking the three or four steps it would take him to get to the opposite side of the bed.

I felt my throat close up as my precious Manon clung to Dutch's hand. I realized then that I was the interloper in the room, not Dutch. Not the man who, only minutes before, had asked what happened between she and I.

I turned and walked out of the room, cursing myself for being such a fool.

—Alegria—

"That wasn't fair, Alegria," Dutch scolded me. "You made him think—"

"That I'd moved on."

"With me."

I caressed the back of his hand with my thumb. "Haven't I?"

"If I believed it's what you really want…"

"It is what I want."

"Listen." Dutch scrubbed his face with his hand. "I know you still love him. You always will."

There was no point in lying; I would always love Mantis, but that didn't mean we could ever be together again. Both of us had said too many things that could never be taken back. I'd given him an ultimatum, and he'd chosen the mission over me.

That's just who Mantis was. From the day I met him, he'd never wavered in his commitment to the Air Force, and then to the CIA. I'd never been first with him, and I'd made it clear that if he wanted me in his life, he had to change his priorities. When he refused, I knew if I didn't end the relationship then, I never would. And I'd be miserable.

"I'm with you now. What I had with him is…over."

"I wish I could believe it was that simple." Dutch shook his head.

"Why are you angry with me?"

He ran one hand through his hair while he grasped my fingers with the other. "Because I saw what just happened. Worse, I felt it."

"You let him leave believing we were together. If you don't want to be with me, why didn't you tell him so?"

Dutch shook his head. "I didn't say I don't want to be with you, Alegria. As to why I didn't try to stop Mantis from leaving, I can't answer that. I guess it's because as much as I care about him, I care about you too, and right now, you need me more."

"I don't want your pity."

Dutch looked away from me. "What do you want?"

I bit my lip. "I…I don't know how to answer that."

He turned back and met my gaze. "Ask me."

"What?"

"Ask me what I want."

"What do you want, Dutch?" I whispered, my eyes filling with tears.

"I want to believe that someday you'll love me half as much as you love Mantis. Just half as much."

He got up and walked out. I knew he'd come back, and when he did, I wasn't sure I'd be able to say anything that would convince him I could love him the way he wanted me to.

2

Zary and Gunner

In just a few days, the people who had saved my life and welcomed me into their makeshift family would be celebrating Thanksgiving. I'd heard of the American holiday but had never been invited to its traditional dinner.

"Good morning, beautiful," said Gunner. He bent over and kissed my forehead.

"Good morning," I murmured.

"Talk to me, Rocket Girl," he said, sitting on the bed next to me. While I'd left behind the code name Raketa, given to me by United Russia, I still loved it when Gunner called me by its English translation.

"Did you work out?" It was a stupid question. He was sweaty and in workout clothes.

"You know I did. Tell me what's on your mind."

I shook my head.

Gunner pushed me over and lay down next to me. "Are you worried about Thanksgiving?"

I smiled. "A little."

"Tell me what worries you the most."

The list was endless. I was meeting Gunner's mother and sister for the first time. And how would it be to spend time with my twin half-sisters? What about my mother and their mother? Would that be awkward? Not to mention that, like me, my mother had never celebrated Thanksgiving before. At least, I doubted she had.

"I have some news on the subject."

More? Now what? When I rubbed my temples, Gunner took my hands in his.

"It's not a big deal. Razor's mother and sister are coming. And his two nieces. They'll stay over at Razor's place."

I did mental math. There were two houses within the compound that sat right on the beach in the seaside village of Cambria. Gunner called the houses a duplex, but no matter how many times he'd tried to explain what that meant, I didn't understand. He even showed me where the garages connected, but to me, they were still two houses.

Whether they were separate houses or a duplex didn't matter as much as the number of bedrooms each one had. Gunner's had three bedrooms, and so far, two of them were occupied. Gunner and I slept in one, and my mother slept in another. When his mother and sister arrived, would they share the unoccupied room?

Razor's house had the same number of bedrooms, and they were quickly filling up too. Ava's twin, Aine, and their mother would soon arrive. If Razor's mother, sister, and nieces came, how would there be room for everyone? Why was I thinking about this? Was it any of my business?

I knew what was really rattling me. I hadn't spent this much time with so many people since my orphanage days, and those weren't memories I wanted to dredge to the surface.

Every day when I woke up, I double-checked my surroundings. If Gunner was still asleep, I'd sneak down the hallway and ease the bedroom door open where my mother slept, just to make sure she was still there.

Seeing her peacefully sleeping was so much like the dreams I'd had for years—that my parents were still alive, and their reported deaths had been a terrible mistake. My father was no longer alive, but I didn't regret his dying. I didn't consider him my father anyway. To me, he was the devil.

When I looked at Gunner, he was studying me. "If you don't talk to me, I can't help solve all those problems rolling around in your head."

I didn't feel well. That was my main problem. Yesterday, the queasiness I'd felt in the morning had gone away by mid-afternoon. I'd been relieved that it didn't last longer, but now it was back.

When I was sick, I wanted to be left alone, but neither Gunner nor my mother had cooperated yesterday. They'd both hovered so much that when I started to feel better, I went for a run on the beach—alone.

"Your mother and I are going shopping in San Luis Obispo this morning. Would you like to join us?"

I smiled. Two days ago, I'd found them in the kitchen, each speaking into his phone and then looking at the screen. "Translation app," he'd explained.

Gunner turned to his side and ran his finger down my cheek. It was something he did often, and it always soothed me.

"Sure, I'll go."

"Come on, get up," he said, pulling my hand.

My stomach rolled like it had the day before. "Wait," I said, taking my hand from his. "I'm not feeling well again."

"I made you breakfast."

The idea of food sent my stomach on another roller-coaster ride. "I can't eat."

"I'll bring it in. Maybe if you try a little…"

Gunner left the room, but was back almost immediately.

"Here we go." He set a tray in front of me with cereal, a banana, and an apple. It wasn't the typical breakfast he usually insisted I ate.

He'd made it his mission to put more "meat on my bones" by making me things to eat, like eggs with bacon or sausage for breakfast and more steak than I'd eaten in my life for dinner.

I had to admit, now that it was in front of me, the simple breakfast looked good.

Gunner sat by my side and peeled a banana he'd brought in for himself.

"You're very happy, considering I'm sick," I said between bites of the cereal I couldn't eat fast enough.

Gunner's face was set in a scowl more often than not, but when he was with me, he smiled a lot. So did I.

"Want some more?" he asked, still smiling.

"Sure, but I can get it."

"Stay where you are. I'll be right back." He took my bowl, and when he returned, he had another banana with him.

"Is that for me?"

Gunner nodded, peeling it and handing it to me.

Ten minutes ago, the idea of eating two bananas would've sent me to the lavatory. I took it from his hand.

"Your mother hasn't heard back, yet, from Topor," he said.

I nodded. Topor, my mother's half brother, would bring a whole other list of worries with him if he decided to join us for the holiday. He hadn't yet responded one way or another.

He'd been tentative with us since the night Petrov died, as though he was relinquishing control of my mother's life to me. So used to having him a constant presence, my mother missed him desperately. His distance frustrated Gunner just as much.

"She told me eating bananas used to make her feel better."

"What do you mean?"

Gunner leaned closer and kissed my forehead. "When she was pregnant with you."

I finished my banana and then took another spoonful of cereal.

"No reaction?"

"To what?" I asked.

"Bananas making her feel better when she was pregnant."

"I don't understand." What kind of reaction was he looking for?

Gunner set a small box on the tray next to my bowl.

"What is that?" I asked. When I read what the box said, my eyes opened wide.

"You figured it out," he said, still smiling from ear to ear.

"No, Gunner. I'm not pregnant."

"What makes you so sure?"

"I can't have children." It was something I knew we'd have to talk about sooner or later, but with as hectic as things had been for us in the last couple of months, it hadn't seemed urgent.

"Why do you think you can't have children?" he asked. His scowl still hadn't returned, as much as I'd expected it to.

"The Russian doctor…"

"They've been known to lie." Gunner scrubbed his face with his hand. "There's something I've been meaning to ask you, though."

"Go ahead."

"The first time…did I…did we…use a condom?"

I nodded. "Condoms. Plural."

"I'm sorry I had to ask, Zary."

"It's okay."

"So…take the test," he said, opening the box and handing me a plastic stick.

I studied it. "What am I supposed to do with this?"

"Pee on it."

"No!" I gasped, grabbing the box from Gunner to read the directions for myself. "I can't believe it," I said, setting the box down.

"It wasn't just your mother who said bananas and cereal made her feel better. Ava said so too."

I looked at the small box a second time. "I didn't think…"

"Go do it, Zary," he murmured.

I was slowly getting used to Gunner calling me by the name only my mother had called me both when I was little, and now too.

"What if…"

Gunner waited for me to finish my sentence, but I didn't know whether to say what if I was pregnant, or what if I wasn't.

"Let's find out and deal with the 'what ifs' later."

He moved and picked up the tray so I could get out of bed.

"I'll be back in a few minutes," he said, walking out of the bedroom.

I studied the plastic stick again. Myself along with the rest of the girls whom the KGB had taken from the orphanage when I was seventeen had been told we couldn't have children. *Sterilized* was the word they'd used at the time.

There was only one of the original eight who had been recruited with me whose name I even remembered. Orina "Losha" Kuznetsov had been my protector and mentor in those early days, but now was in hiding even though the bounty United Russia had on her head had been lifted.

Even if she weren't, I doubted Losha would welcome me reaching out simply to ask whether she knew if the KGB had really sterilized us.

I went into the lavatory, followed the instructions, and waited.

—*Gunner*—

"How is she feeling?" Ava asked.

"Better with food in her stomach."

Ava had something else on her mind, but I didn't want to ask what it was. If I did, she'd tell me, and what I really wanted to do was get back to Zary and see what the stick showed.

"Hey, man," said my best friend, Razor, Ava's husband, who came up and hugged his wife from behind. "What's shakin'?"

For a guy with the level of intelligence I knew Razor possessed, my friend's flippant behavior grated on my nerves sometimes.

"Nothing," I grumbled, walking back into the bedroom. I didn't see Zary right away, so I peeked into the bathroom. She was sitting on the edge of the bathtub, staring at the pregnancy test.

"Well?" I asked, walking over to her.

Instead of answering, she handed him the stick that she'd wrapped in tissue.

"What does this mean?"

She moved the box closer to me.

"Zary?"

She turned and looked at me for the first time since I came into the room.

"They lied."

I couldn't tell whether the positive result made her happy or sad. If it was the latter, I didn't want to make it worse by telling her that, at this moment, I was the happiest man who'd ever lived.

She stood, walked past me, and sat on the edge of the bed. I watched as she pulled the t-shirt she wore to bed over her head and then stood to take off her panties before reaching her hand out to mine.

"I'm sweaty," I told her, pulling my shirt over my head like she had.

"I don't care."

I slid off my shorts and got in bed, next to her. "I wish you'd tell me what you're thinking," I whispered before nuzzling her neck with kisses.

"I don't want to talk, Gunner."

I was all for what she wanted to do instead, but something felt off. I sat up and pulled her into my arms so her head rested on my chest.

"All these years that you didn't think you could have children, and now you're pregnant. It's a lot to take in."

Her arm tightened around my waist, but she didn't respond.

"Zary, do you want to have a baby?"

"I don't know."

3

Ava and Razor

—*Razor*—

"I know she's pregnant," Ava whispered when Gunner walked away. "But it's early for her to talk about it. I mean, I'm not even comfortable talking about it yet."

"Outta my element here, Avarie," I told her. How would I know when she would be?

"You aren't really supposed to say anything until after the first trimester is over. You know, just in case."

"Just in case of what?"

"A miscarriage."

"Right," I said, remembering now that my sister had told me the same thing when she was pregnant with her first little girl.

I pulled Ava over to the sofa and onto my lap. "When can we talk about it?" I asked, putting my hand on her belly.

"Christmas."

Whether anyone else knew didn't matter to me; all I cared about was that my wife was happy, healthy, and safe. "I may have told someone I shouldn't have," I confessed. "Actually, that would be plural."

"I know, Tabon. I was at Doc and Merrigan's too, remember?"

I loved it when she called me by the name I'd hated most of my life. From her lips, it sounded as sweet as honey.

"Who have you told?" I asked.

"The same number of people you have. Maybe a couple more."

"So, I'm not in trouble?"

Ava smiled and rested her head on my shoulder. "Do you think they'll get married?"

"Yeah, I do. I know Gunner wants to marry Zary."

Ava sat back and looked into my eyes. "Did he tell you that?"

I leaned forward and kissed her. "I don't want to talk about Gunner and Zary anymore. I want to talk about you and me."

"I loved our wedding," she murmured.

Weddings weren't exactly what I wanted to talk about. I'd rather talk about our wedding night.

"It all went so fast…"

"Do you regret getting married the way we did?" I asked, sliding my hand under her shirt and toying with her nipple. I loved how sensitive they were because of the pregnancy, and the little gasps of pleasure I could coax from her just by gently nibbling on them.

Ava took a deep breath and melted further into me. Her cheeks flushed pink, and her pretty eyes hooded.

"I need you, baby," I said, lifting her in my arms and carrying her out Gunner's front door and into mine.

Loving Ava was the best part of my life. I'd never imagined that I could be as happy as I was, or that I'd feel so complete. And the baby? My heart swelled every time I thought about my child growing inside my beloved wife.

I kicked the front door closed behind me and carried Ava up the stairs to our bedroom. Every day, the whole house looked more like a home as she added her touch to each of the professionally decorated rooms. None more than our bedroom, though. Somehow she'd managed to make the Japanese-themed decor look both masculine and feminine.

Her eyes closed, and her face flushed the pretty pink I loved so much as I undressed her.

—Ava—

"Tabon," I pleaded, reaching for him.

"I've got you, baby," he said, using his knee to gently part my thighs so he could settle between them.

When I'd first realized I was pregnant, Tabon was worried about making love to me, afraid doing so would somehow hurt the baby. After we'd gone to my first doctor's appointment and she'd reassured us that having sex was perfectly okay, and encouraged, Tabon diligently made up for lost time.

"God, you feel good," he groaned as he slid inside my wetness.

"I love you so much," I murmured.

Tabon pulled back and looked into my eyes. "I love you, Avarie."

"What was that?" I asked when Tabon stilled.

"Doorbell. I'd tell you to ignore it, but my guess is that it's your mother and sister, since no one else has the new gate code."

I clung to him as he moved my arm from around his torso. *"No,"* I cried, knowing I had to let go but wishing I could tell my mother and sister to go away.

He tossed my clothes on the bed while he dressed.

"I'll go let them in," he said as he rushed out of our bedroom.

"Don't let them come upstairs," I hollered after him.

Sitting up, I grabbed my sweater and pulled it over my head, all the while mumbling curse words. I'd just pulled on my jeans and was about to get up when the bedroom door opened.

"Sorry, Sis," Aine said, coming to sit next to me. "Bad timing?"

"I told him not to let you come up here," I grumbled. "How's Mom?"

"Pissed, but okay."

Not only had our mother found out her first husband—and our father—wasn't the man she'd thought she married all those years ago, her second husband had asked for a divorce once they found out who husband number one really was.

"It isn't her fault," I said.

"But who wants to be married to a guy who thinks it is?"

"Good point."

"There's something I want to talk to you about."

"Sure." I leaned closer to my twin.

"There's someone I'd like to invite to Thanksgiving dinner."

I clapped my hands. "Really? Who? This is so exciting? How long have you been seeing this mystery person? Oh my God, my sister is in love!"

"Slow down, cowgirl. It's very new."

"I don't believe you. You wouldn't invite someone you'd just started seeing to a family holiday."

"I would if he knows everyone who will be here."

I sat back, quickly zipping through the other K19 Security Solutions team members. "It isn't Monk, is it?"

"No." Aine scrunched her eyes "Why?"

"I think Tabon's sister has a thing for him."

"That would be awkward, but no, it isn't Monk."

"Don't make me guess. Just tell me who it is."

Aine bit her lip.

"Just tell me," I said again.

"Okay…Griffin."

Griffin? Who in the hell was Griffin? "Wait," I gasped. "Do you mean Striker?"

Aine's worried expression confirmed my guess.

"Of course," I exclaimed, hoping my over-the-top happy response fooled my sister. I should've known better.

"Nobody likes him," Aine pouted.

"That isn't true. I like him."

"What about Razor?"

I wasn't sure. Tabon was fairly good-natured, but I'd heard him complain about Striker a few times. The bigger issue would be with Gunner, who had made no secret of his feelings for the former CIA agent.

"Let me talk to him."

"Who?"

"I'll start with Tabon. Have you already invited him?"

"No, but…"

"What?"

"He doesn't have anywhere else to go."

"Did he tell you that?"

"Not exactly. He asked me to go away with him."

"Come on," I said, pulling my sister off the bed. "Let's go make it official."

"What does that mean?"

"We aren't going to ask. We're going to tell my husband *and* his best friend that you've invited your boyfriend to dinner."

—Razor—

I smiled as Ava and her sister came downstairs. She and her twin were up to something; I could tell by the glint in her eyes.

"Hi, Mom," she said, walking over to her mother.

"I was just telling Razor that we've booked rooms at the bed and breakfast on Moonstone Beach."

"Which one? You know there are at least twenty."

"I don't know. Moonstone something or other."

Ava laughed. "That doesn't narrow it down, Mom."

"Cambria Shores," murmured Aine, who was looking at her phone.

I noticed that she was biting her lower lip. Ava did that when she was worried about something too.

"What's up?" I asked, putting my arm around my wife's twin.

"Nothing," she answered, locking the screen, and shoving her phone into her back pocket.

I looked at Ava, who was also absentmindedly chewing her lip.

"Okay, you two. Tell me what's going on."

"Aine wants to invite Griffin to Thanksgiving dinner," blurted their mother.

I looked back and forth between the sisters. "Striker?"

Ava nodded.

"Uh…sure…uh…"

"Never mind. It isn't a big—"

"Wait," said Ava. "It is a big deal." Her eyes met mine, and she put her hand on her hip. "If she can't invite him, she won't be spending Thanksgiving with us."

I held up my hands. "I didn't say she couldn't."

"You were going to," she pouted.

I walked over and put my arm around her shoulders. "No. I wasn't. He's more than welcome to join us."

From the corner of my eye, I saw Aine's tentative smile.

"Don't you need to ask Gunner?"

"Nope," I answered, hoping Ava didn't pick up on my fib.

"Razor," she threatened, letting me know she had. She only called me Razor when she was pissed at me about something, and lying was at the top of what made her mad.

"I'm not going to ask," I told her. "I'm going to tell him as a courtesy."

The three women standing with me in the kitchen all laughed.

"Yeah. Okay. I get it. I'll be right back."

I rapped on Gunner's front door, hoping my friend wouldn't pitch a fit when I told him about Aine wanting to invite Striker to dinner.

"What?" he barked when he opened the door.

"Hey," I answered, pushing past him.

"We were just leaving."

I saw Zary and her mother standing near the door to the garage.

"I came over to tell you to add one more for dinner."

Gunner raised his eyebrows and scowled. "Who?"

"Striker."

"No—"

"Aine invited him."

I waited while Gunner processed through what I'd just said.

"Why?"

"Evidently, they're…uh…seeing each other."

"Tell her to stop! *Jesus.* Striker? What's wrong with her, is she blind?"

I smiled when Zary came up and put one hand on Gunner's chest and her other arm around his waist.

"He isn't that bad," she murmured.

"Yeah, he is."

Zary stood on her toes and whispered something I couldn't hear.

Gunner looked at her for a few seconds and then turned to me, gritting his teeth. "The more, the merrier."

"That's what I told her you'd say." I chuckled and slapped Gunner's back.

I could still hear him muttering something I didn't try hard to understand as I walked back out the front door.

—Ava—

"What did he say?" I asked when Tabon walked back into the kitchen.

"More the merrier."

I studied my husband's face, but he wasn't lying. "Love must agree with him."

He smiled. "Somethin' like that."

"We should go check in," Aine said to our mother.

Peggy looked at her watch. "It's early."

"Let's go for a walk on the beach, then."

"Honey, I'd rather—"

Aine's face tightened, and she motioned toward Tabon and me. "I think they want to be alone."

"It's okay," I said, but Aine shook her head.

"We need to go check in."

I shrugged. "Suit yourself," I said, kissing my sister's cheek first and then my mother's. "Should we plan to get together for dinner later?"

"I'll let you know," Aine answered while our mother looked at her with a stunned expression.

"What was that all about?" Tabon asked when my mom and Aine were gone.

"I'm not sure. Maybe Striker is trying to reach her."

Tabon nodded. "Wanna pick up where we left off, or is the moment over?"

I smiled. "The moment is never over with you, my hotter-than-all-get-out husband."

"I like the way you think."

Tabon picked me up and carried me upstairs, like he had earlier.

"I can walk, you know."

"I know, but why would I let you when having you in my arms feels so damn good?"

"What do you think about this thing between Aine and Striker?" I asked when we got upstairs.

"Haven't given it a thought, and I don't plan to. I have other, more important, things on my mind," he said as he undressed me for the second time.

"I just—"

Tabon put two fingers on my lips. "Shh. Can't you hear the music?" He started to hum. "You don't want to turn the music off. Do you, baby?"

I smiled. "Never."

"That's what I thought. Now remind me where I was before we were so rudely interrupted."

I spread my legs when Tabon rested his hands on my knees.

"That's right. You remember."

4

Aine and Striker

—*Aine*—

"Why were you in such a hurry?" my mother asked. "We can't check in for another three hours."

"I got us an early check-in."

I loved my mother and enjoyed spending time with her, particularly since she was sober and had stopped insisting that Ava and I call her "Peggy." Right now, though, all I cared about was getting her situated in her room so I could get ready for Griffin's arrival.

"You're very anxious to get rid of me," my mother said when I carried the bags to her room. We were staying on the Central Coast of California for a week, yet my mother had packed three heavy bags.

"What's in here?" I asked, regretting it as soon as I had. I didn't care if my mother brought boulders as long as she hurried up.

"I guess the tide has turned," Peggy said with tears in her eyes.

"What is that supposed to mean?"

"There was a time when I couldn't wait to drop you and your sister off at boarding school."

I took a deep breath. When had our mother ever dropped us off at school? From what I remembered, she got Ava and I as far as the train station before she wished us "*bon voyage*."

"Mom, I—"

"It isn't necessary to explain. I'm just thankful you and your sister want to spend any time at all with me."

"Please don't do this now," I begged. "I'm sorry. It's just that Griffin is…"

When my mother smiled, I lost my train of thought.

"I'm so happy for you, sweetheart," Peggy said, cupping my face.

"I don't want everyone making too much of this. I'm inviting him to join us for Thanksgiving dinner. That's it."

"If I'm not mistaken, today is Monday."

I sighed. "And?"

"Thanksgiving isn't for another four days."

"Okay, he's driving up today. He's in Montecito, meeting with Doc and Merrigan, and it didn't make sense for him to fly back to Virginia only to turn around and fly back here."

"Mmm hmm." My mother's smile widened.

"Mom! *Seriously.*"

My phone buzzed in my pocket, which did not go unnoticed by my mother.

"Answer it," she said, pushing me out the door of the room.

"I'll talk to you later, okay?"

My mom smiled again and nodded before she closed the door in my face.

"Hi," I said.

"You sound out of breath."

"My mom…it's a long story. Anyway, hi."

"Hi. I miss you."

My cheeks flushed. "I miss you too."

"What's the plan? Am I driving up to Cambria, or are you flying down to Santa Barbara?"

"You're driving."

"You're sure about this."

"Razor told me that Gunner said the more, the merrier."

"Did he realize I'm part of the *more*?"

"He knows that you *are* the more."

"The man can't stand me."

"That's what everyone says. I think that's the way Gunner wants it. If you think he doesn't like you, you're less apt to try to start a conversation with him."

Griffin laughed. "He's an ornery bastard."

"He seems happier now that he and Zary are together."

"Zary. That'll take some getting used to. I've only ever known her as Raketa."

"Don't call her that, especially in front of Gunner."

Griffin laughed again. "What's with everyone deciding they don't want to be called by their code names anymore?"

"I call you Griffin. Would you rather I called you Striker?"

"Aine." I could tell he was smiling. "I will answer to Rover if it's from your lips."

"Hmm. I kind of like that. Okay, Rover, when will you be here?"

"Two hours tops. Text me the address."

—Striker—

I disconnected the call and threw the phone on the passenger seat of my rental car. I'd splurged and rented a convertible Mercedes, hoping Aine and I could take a drive up to Big Sur in it, maybe farther. I was thinking about asking her if she'd let me drive her home after the holiday. From the Central Coast to Yachats, Oregon, would be a breathtakingly beautiful drive, and it would give us more time alone together.

As for my splurge on the car, the money I was making as a K19 partner allowed me to have a little fun after getting by on CIA pay for so many years. It wasn't that they didn't pay well; it was just that the money I made with K19 was so much more than I'd ever dreamed possible.

I was considering putting my condo in McLean on the market. I wasn't sure I'd be there that often anyway. With my new tax bracket, I could afford something new. Maybe something closer to Yachats—and Aine.

I scrubbed my face as traffic slowed to a crawl, trying not to overthink this thing with Aine or what kind of reception I was going to get from Gunner Godet.

The first time we met, I knew Gunner didn't like me. Ever since, I'd worked hard to get the guy to give me an inch, to no avail. I'd even talked to Fatale about it.

"Can you put in a good word for me with Paps?" I'd asked.

"I can, but it won't do any good," she'd responded. "He doesn't like anyone from what I can tell."

"He likes you."

"He tolerates me."

"It's worse with me. He hates me."

Fatale's advice had been to stay out of Gunner's way, which hadn't worked too well considering the last op we'd done was to rescue Zary, the woman Gunner was in love with. Hard to stay out of someone's way when they want your help saving the love of their life.

I scanned the satellite radio stations and thought about Aine instead of the man who would likely never accept me into his small circle of friends.

I'd never forgotten the day I met her at a wedding I still wasn't sure I'd been invited to, but had gone to anyway.

***

"This is a bad idea," I said to Monk.

"You're part of the team."

"It isn't official yet. And even if I am, that doesn't mean Razor wants me at his wedding."

Monk didn't say anything else, which didn't surprise me. The man said as few words as possible.

I was halfway down the steps to the beach, considering turning around and going back to my car, when I saw *her.*

I recognized the woman. She was Ava McNamara's twin, Aine, and she took my breath away. With her tan skin, sandy blonde hair, and curves that made my mouth water, she looked like the quintessential California girl. I knew better, though; she'd been raised on the East Coast.

As I got closer and our eyes met, I saw that hers were deep blue, like the ocean.

The brief ceremony, during which her sister and Razor Sharp were married, became a blur. I wasn't able to keep my eyes off of Aine.

"Hi," I said, intercepting her as she walked between clusters of people.

She put her hand on her heart.

"I'm sorry. I didn't mean to startle you." I held out my hand. "I'm Striker."

"I'm Aine." She put her hand in mine to shake. "It's nice to meet you…uh…Striker."

"Actually, it's Griffin. Griffin Ellis."

"Right," she said, motioning toward Razor, Gunner, and some of the other guys. "You all have special names."

"Code names, although I'm not sure there's anything special about them."

"I like Griffin."

"Thanks. I like Aine."

She smiled, her cheeks flushed, and she looked at her hand still clasped in mine, but she didn't try to pull away.

"Do you know if there will be dancing later?" God, had I really just asked her that? There had to be fewer than thirty people standing on the sand, most barefooted. I wondered if they'd even have food.

"Actually, there will be."

"Food?"

"No." She laughed. "Dancing. Are you hungry?"

"Maybe a little. I can go grab something—"

"Come with me," she said, pulling me by the hand that was still holding hers.

"Where are we going?"

"Kitchen. It's this place where they have...*food*."

Damn, she was even prettier when she smiled.

"What?" she asked when I didn't move, but didn't let go of her hand either.

"You're beautiful," I murmured, getting closer to her.

"Thanks. You're not so bad yourself."

***

We'd made peanut butter and jelly sandwiches that day, and then sat on the deck and chatted about what was happening on the beach below us.

Between then and now, I'd only seen her twice, but we talked every chance we got. With me traveling back and forth between the States and Azerbaijan, it hadn't been easy to keep in touch, but now that the mission was over, I was looking forward to time off for the holidays. If she'd have me, I planned to spend every minute I could with Aine.

The traffic opened up, and I sped up the highway, wishing I'd taken a commuter jet instead. After waiting so long to see her, the last couple of hours were killer.

—Aine—

I changed my clothes three times, opened a bottle of wine, had a glass, and then changed my clothes again.

Today was the day Griffin and I would finally have more than a couple of stolen hours together. In fact, if things went as planned, we'd be together all week. I bit my lip, wondering if the attraction would be as strong once our time together was open-ended. It wasn't like we were slowly easing into it; we were pulling the throttle wide open.

Seeing I had at least an hour before he arrived, I decided to take a walk on the beach. At least that would keep me from changing my clothes again.

The sun was shining, but it was still cold on the Central Coast. Oregon, where my mother and I had settled once Ava announced that she and Razor planned to live there full time, was just as cold, if not colder.

When I started out, I wondered if I'd be too warm in my flannel-lined jeans and Fair Isle turtleneck, but now I was glad I'd thought to grab my barn jacket too.

As I walked, the sun's light would shine on small pieces of rock, making me shield my eyes from the glare. I knelt and picked up one of the smooth, round stones and studied it, mesmerized by what looked like billowy clouds of blue and white atop a moonlight sheen. Moonstones, I thought as I put several in my pocket along with blue and green sea glass, sand dollars, and shells so delicate it was hard to believe they'd stayed in one piece as the ocean washed them onshore.

With pockets almost full, I stood to walk back up the beach. I hadn't seen a single person since I started out, but now I saw one—a man—walking toward me.

I picked up my pace when, as I got closer, I realized the man was Griffin. I kept myself from running toward him, until I saw him break into a jog.

When we came together, he picked me up and swung me in a circle.

"Do you know how happy I am to see you?" He rested his forehead against mine and set me back on my feet. "Can I kiss you?"

Instead of answering, I kissed him.

Griffin tightened his embrace and thrust his tongue inside my mouth when I opened to him. The intense passion of his kiss left me dizzy, and I clung to him.

"How did you know where to find me?" I asked, out of breath.

"You forget what I do for a living."

"Seriously?" I pulled back from him.

"No. I asked your mom."

I laughed. "Okay, I'll bite. How did you find her?"

"She found me. I got the impression she was anticipating my arrival."

"I'm so sorry."

He rested his forehead against mine again. "Don't be. I found you faster than I would've, which means I have more time for this."

Griffin covered my mouth with his and held me so tight. With anyone else, I might've had a hard time breathing, but I'd waited so long to be in his arms that getting air into my lungs didn't seem to matter much.

—Striker—

"Is there anything special you want to do tonight?" she asked as we walked back to the inn hand in hand.

There were many special things I wanted to do, but I refrained from listing them in detail. "Dinner?" I asked instead. "I heard that place is pretty good." I pointed to a restaurant a few doors down from the inn.

"I love that place, and it shouldn't be busy since it's Monday."

"I haven't checked to see if the inn has any rooms available yet."

Aine stopped walking momentarily. "Oh," she said before continuing on.

"Hold on," I said. "I didn't want to assume."

Aine's cheeks flamed, and she tried to look away from me, but I held her chin with my hand.

"Are you inviting me to stay with you?"

"I…um…yeah. I guess so."

"You guess so?" I smiled and then leaned forward to kiss her. "Maybe this will help convince you."

5

Mantis, Alegria, Dutch

—Mantis—

I zipped up my bag and was about to hoist it over my shoulder when I heard a knock at the door. I peered out the window, saw who it was, and considered pretending I wasn't home. However, both my motorcycle and car were parked on the street in front of the condo I'd rented in the same complex where, unbeknown to me at the time I'd signed the short-term lease, Dutch was also living temporarily.

"I know you're in there. Open up," shouted the man who, until recently, had been my best friend.

"Leave me the fuck alone," I muttered before unlocking and opening the door.

"I heard that," said Dutch, pushing his way inside and eyeing the duffel bag. "Where you headed?"

"Connecticut," I lied.

"Seriously?"

"What do you want?" I was in no mood for questioning from anyone, let alone Dutch.

"Alegria is getting out of the hospital today."

"Glad to hear it." I had no intention of admitting to Dutch that I already knew she was.

"She's doing a lot better."

"I wish her all the best."

"Look, what happened…"

"Is there another reason you stopped by?"

"Mantis, come on, we're best friends."

"Who aren't seventeen anymore. We don't hang out. What do you want, Dutch?"

"She told me it was over between the two of you."

"What is this? Are you here to ask my forgiveness for being in a relationship with my *ex*-girlfriend? Or is it permission you're after? Get over yourself, neither of you is that important."

"You don't have to be an asshole about it."

I shook my head. "Alegria and I had a thing. It's over. Both of us have moved on. How does that make me an asshole?" I looked at my phone. "I need to get to the airfield. Was there anything else?"

Dutch looked out the window and then back at me. "Happy Thanksgiving."

"Same to you. Now, if you don't mind…"

Dutch walked out the door, leaving me feeling exactly like the asshole my friend had accused me of being. Maybe I was, but why did Dutch have to get involved with the one woman I knew would always own me? Weren't there four billion other women in the world he could've chosen from?

Maybe I should take that into consideration myself. Given the astronomical number, surely I could find another woman to love heart and soul.

I checked the time again. At Gunner's request, I was piloting K19's commuter jet up to San Luis Obispo from the airfield in Santa Barbara. The only reason time was an issue was because the private plane section of the regional airport was especially busy near the holidays. My flight plan was filed, and if I didn't get there on time, it might be several hours before I could get another slot.

I was glad now that I'd called Gunner. I'd told the man I was calling to check on Raketa—who was going by Zary now—but was elated when Gunner asked what my plans were for Thanksgiving. It was precisely the reason I'd called.

"I'm a man without a mission," I'd told him.

Gunner had laughed. "You're welcome to come here. We're opening a zoo, it appears. All the single animals will be here this week."

"I appreciate the invitation."

"By the way," he'd said. "Striker will be here too."

That made sense, he was one of the mateless animals. Unlike Dutch and Alegria.

I'd thanked him again and then booked a room at the inn Gunner recommended.

—Dutch—

"If Alegria is able to ride in a car for a couple of hours, you're both welcome to join us here. We're in Cambria for Thanksgiving, not Oregon," Razor told me.

"I appreciate it."

"No problem. You're both K19 family. In fact, the two of you should stay here at the house. She'll be more comfortable than she would be at the inn."

I thanked him again, hung up, and went into the guest bedroom to check on her. She'd been in relatively good spirits when we left the hospital, but once we arrived at the condo I'd rented, she told me she was exhausted and wanted to rest. That was six hours ago, and she was still asleep.

I wasn't sure what I'd expected from Mantis when I stopped by before going to pick her up. Maybe I was looking for some sign that we were still friends. I sure didn't feel like we were.

I'd had a flicker of hope that Mantis would be open to spending Thanksgiving with Alegria and me, but I should've known better. It would hurt far too much to spend the holiday with the woman he loved when he believed she was with another man. I knew firsthand; I'd spent many holidays with Alegria and Mantis when they were together.

I'd been able to bury my feelings for years because Alegria had never been mine. She still wasn't, not really. She was too stubborn to admit she wanted Mantis back in her life, but one day she would, and that would leave me the odd man out. One would think that knowing it was an inevitability, I'd walk away now, but I couldn't bring myself to leave her.

—Alegria—

I tried to roll over, but my body didn't want to cooperate. I needed a pain pill, but didn't want to ask Dutch to bring one to me.

If I'd been cleared to travel by plane, I would've flown to France and recuperated at my parents' house, but that long of a flight was out of the question so soon after my surgery—the outcome of which was far better than the doctors had initially hoped.

The damage to my spinal cord was significant enough that they'd told me, going in, that I may have long-term paralysis. When I came to, I could move all her extremities without any difficulty. The kind of pain I was experiencing now, however, they'd warned might be a constant in my life from now on.

Instead of feeling sorry for myself—and I was—I should be thankful I wasn't paralyzed.

Without realizing how dead-on the random shot he'd fired had been, Petrov had hit me in the back as I was walking away. If I'd been facing his direction, his bullet likely would've killed me.

"Mon coeur." The words Mantis had said to me when I woke from surgery echoed in my head. How lovely they'd sounded, coming from his lips, but what had I done? As soon as I realized Dutch was in the room too, I'd reached out to him, essentially pounding the last nail into the coffin that had once been my life with the man who would hold my heart forever.

"You're awake," said Dutch, opening the door to the room.

"Yes."

"Time for some pain relief."

He handed me a white pill and a glass of water.

"Merci," I murmured.

"You need more rest," he said, stroking my forehead.

"What time is it?"

"A little after two in the afternoon."

"The pain…"

"I know. Rest." He leaned down and kissed my cheek. "I'll be back to check on you in a bit. If you need anything else, ring the bell."

"Wait. Dutch?"

He was almost through the bedroom door but came back to the bedside.

"Have you…"

"Ask the question, sweetheart."

"Does Mantis know I'm out of the hospital?"

"He does."

I nodded.

"I'll be back later."

He left the room and closed the door behind him. Had I hurt his feelings by asking about Mantis? Why had I, anyway?

—*Mantis*—

The flight had been quick and easy. The plane was now parked in the hangar at the San Luis Obispo airfield, and soon I'd be in a rental car on my way to Cambria. Any temptation I had to see Alegria would be thwarted by distance.

The drive was as easy as the flight had been; there was virtually no traffic. I guessed that later in the week I wouldn't have been so lucky.

I pulled into the inn's parking lot and walked over to the office to check in.

"Are you here for the holiday?" asked the woman behind the front desk.

"I am."

"We have an unusually high number of guests this year who are. In fact, we're fully booked like the rest of the inns on Moonstone Beach."

I nodded. "I got lucky."

"You did. A man just called, wanting a room, and we had to turn him away."

Not interested in further small talk, I didn't respond until she handed me my room key and I thanked her.

"I didn't know you'd be here too," said Striker, walking past the office with a woman who looked familiar. "Happy Thanksgiving. Mantis, you know Aine McNamara, don't you?"

"Yes," I said, reaching out to shake her hand. "Happy Thanksgiving to you both."

"I guess we'll catch up with you later," said Striker, walking toward one of the rooms, holding Aine's hand in his.

"Sure thing," I murmured, but they were already too far away to hear me.

Striker and the McNamara twin? When had that begun? I shook my head. It really wasn't any of my business. If my chest didn't hurt with loneliness, I probably wouldn't have given the two of them a second thought.

Maybe coming to Cambria for the holiday hadn't been such a good idea. I couldn't have stomached being the third wheel between Alegria and Dutch, but this might be just as bad. What if I was the only single guy here?

—Dutch—

I scrubbed my face with my hand, lamenting my relationship with Alegria for the thousandth time. If I hadn't walked into the bar that night and found her drunk enough that I knew I had to take her home, maybe the thing that should never have started between us, wouldn't have.

If I were a better man, I never would've slept with her in the first place. Instead, I was the shithead who had lusted after and longed for my best friend's girlfriend for years. When the opportunity presented itself, I'd swept in like a goddamn vulture.

Having her in my bed had been like a dream come true. No matter how many times my conscience told me I should end it, I hadn't been able to.

"Hey, you," I said, surprised to see Alegria walking into the kitchen.

"Hi. I thought maybe I should eat something."

"Of course. Have a seat, and I'll heat up some soup. Sound good?"

She nodded and looked out the window.

"Thanksgiving is in three days. We've been invited up to Cambria to have dinner with Razor, Gunner, and the rest of the crew."

"Okay."

"Sound good?"

"Sure. Who else will be there?"

"I don't know, exactly, but my guess is you're asking about Mantis, and he won't be. He's going to Connecticut." I set the steaming bowl of soup in front of her and watched as she took three spoonfuls and then rested the spoon on the side of the bowl.

"I'm not as hungry as I thought."

"You can have more later."

Alegria shuffled back to the bedroom, leaving me wondering if the news about Mantis being on the East Coast for Thanksgiving had ruined her appetite.

—Alegria—

The first Thanksgiving I spent in America was at Mantis' parents' house in Connecticut. He'd invited me to go along when he realized that, as an international student, I'd be staying at the academy with a handful of other people for the holiday.

***

I was nervous on the flight, and he reassured me.

"My parents are really nice. You don't have to worry. They've always been great about me inviting friends to the house," he said.

"Is that what we are, Cadet Cassman?"

"What would you like us to be, Cadet Mondreau?" He smiled, leaned closer, and kissed me.

Later that night, Mantis sneaked into the room where I was sleeping, and I'd lost my virginity.

***

From that trip on, we'd been a couple. Sure, we'd broken up and gotten back together several times after we graduated. There were times I thought we'd never speak again, like I did now. We'd always wound up back together, though. Would this be the one time we didn't?

6

Zary and Gunner

—Zary—

"We aren't eating until four. You'll feel better by then. Don't worry—your mom, my mom, and I got this."

I smiled. There were so many things I loved about Gunner, but none more than how he was with my mother.

Little by little, they left the translation app behind and communicated in a mix of English and Azeri. Today, Gunner and his mom, Madeline, were teaching my mom how to make stuffing for the turkey. I could hear him asking her to read the ingredients out loud. She struggled, but Madeline helped her sound out the words.

We were responsible for bringing the turkeys over to Razor's while other guests pitched in with side dishes and pies. At least that's what Gunner had told me was happening.

Our combined guest list had grown to a number I was unsure of, but most were staying at inns along Moonstone Beach rather than at the duplex. Even Gunner's sister had opted to stay at one of the inns so their mother could stay at the house.

Every morning, Gunner brought a tray in with a bowl of cereal and a banana; the only thing I could keep down before noon.

"I can get it myself," I'd say again and again.

"Let me take care of you," Gunner responded each time.

"Good morning," Madeline said, poking her head in the bedroom doorway.

I smiled. Gunner's mother was one of the nicest people I'd ever met, exhibiting no signs that Gunner inherited his grouchiness from her. His sister, Odette, was just as nice.

"Good morning."

"How are you feeling?"

"Better," I said, waving my hand over the breakfast tray Gunner had delivered.

"I can take that if you're finished."

"I can get it." I started to get up.

"Let us take care of you," Madeline said, making me smile. "What?" she asked.

"That's what Gunner always says. I should get up anyway."

"I remember feeling the same way you do when I was pregnant. I'll tell you what my mother told me."

"What is that?"

"Once this baby is born, you'll no longer be able to stay in bed when you don't feel well. For eighteen years, maybe longer, you'll have to take care of someone else before yourself. Rest, relax, and sleep while you can."

"Thank you," I murmured. I understood Madeline's words, but before Gunner, it had been a very long time since anyone had taken care of me. It was a difficult concept to get used to, especially coming from so many people.

In addition to Gunner and his mother, my own mother, Odette, and even Ava and Aine fussed over me.

"I don't know why I feel so tired," I confessed to Madeline. "I feel like all I've done is sleep."

"That's because your baby is sapping everything he or she needs from your body," said Ava, joining Madeline in the bedroom's doorway.

"You're both welcome to come in…"

"I need to go check on Gunner, your mom, and the turkeys. I'll take your tray and come back a little later," said Madeline.

"You're sure I'm not intruding?" asked Ava.

"Definitely not." I pulled the covers up and tucked my arms under them.

"Are you cold?" Ava asked.

"A little."

"This is one of the things I love about this place. Tabon and I have a fireplace in the bedroom too." Ava flipped a switch. "This will help. It is chilly in here."

"Thank you."

"Is there anything else you need?"

I smiled again. "You're pregnant too."

"I'm further along than you are, though."

"Doesn't that mean you should be more tired than I am?"

Ava smiled too, and then studied me.

"What?"

"Sometimes I feel like I'm looking in a mirror, and then at other times, I don't think we look anything alike."

"I've seen it too."

"You have?"

"You sound surprised."

"I wonder if…maybe I'm pushing you too hard."

"I'm sorry."

"No, don't be." Ava gasped. "I didn't say that to make you feel bad."

"I haven't had a lot of female…relationships. I haven't had many relationships at all."

"Your life hasn't been easy."

My chest tightened. "Yours hasn't been either. Gunner told me about the boarding school."

"Yeah. Although, I had Aine."

"Yes. I'm sorry about your father."

"Did you think of him that way?"

"No."

"Neither did we. It's like our dad died before Petrov did. Does that make sense?"

"It does. My father died when I was a small child."

"Your mom is very nice."

Willing my tears away, I closed my eyes and rested my head against the pillow.

"It's okay to cry," Ava whispered.

When I opened my eyes, Ava was crying too.

"I'm sorry," I said again.

"Please don't be." Ava sat on the side of the bed. "Would you mind if I hugged you?"

I shook my head. "I'd like that."

"Hey, what about me?" I heard someone say.

Ava and I looked up and saw Aine had come into the room.

"Get over here, girl," Ava told her sister, pulling her into our hug.

—Gunner—

"Can I help?"

I looked up from chopping celery and saw Striker standing in my kitchen. I stifled a groan.

"You can do the onions," I grunted at the man.

Striker laughed and walked over to the sink to wash his hands.

"Who's this?" asked my mom.

"Mom, meet Striker," I said without looking up.

I rolled my eyes when I heard my mom say, "Nice to meet you."

"I'm not your son's favorite person," Striker told her.

"Knock it off," I grumbled. "I don't like anyone."

"Except Zary," said my mom.

"No, Mom. I don't like Zary; I love her. And I love you too." I kissed her cheek.

"See? He can be sweet."

I pointed to the pile of onions. "Get busy," I told Striker before getting back to chopping the celery.

"What's wrong?" I heard my mother say.

I looked up to see Zary's mom join us; she was crying.

Even if I'd gotten my translation app turned on in time to catch what she was saying, I doubted it would've picked much up as emotional as she was.

I watched as she pointed down the hall and was about to bound to my bedroom when I heard her say, *"Sisters."*

"Oh," cried my mom, whose own eyes filled with tears.

I set the knife down, walked down the hallway, and looked inside the room in time to see Zary, Ava, and Aine hugging.

"Damn," I heard Striker mumble from behind me and turned around to see him wiping a tear away.

As tempted as I was to give the man shit about it, I didn't. It was a beautiful moment to witness.

"How long has it been goin' on?" I asked once we were back in the kitchen.

"It hasn't. Not really. We met at Ava and Razor's wedding."

"But she invited you to Thanksgiving dinner."

"We're giving it a go."

"Be careful, Striker. She's family."

"I really like her, Gunner."

"Yeah, whatever. Get to work."

A few minutes later, my mom came back into the kitchen with Zary's mother, Svetlana, who walked over and showed me her phone.

Rauf will be here tomorrow was written on the screen.

"That's good," I responded, not knowing what else to say, especially when the woman smiled.

Life had certainly turned into a shitstorm of weirdness in the last six months, and there was nothing I could do but go along for the ride. Former CIA agents were hanging out with former Russian assassins; people I'd never dreamed would be standing in my kitchen were, and the woman I loved more than life itself was in the bedroom with my baby growing inside of her.

When I'd talked to Zary about her saying she wasn't sure she wanted to have a baby, she told me that wasn't what she meant.

"I'm not saying I don't. I'm saying I don't know how to feel, Gunner."

"But you want to *have* the baby?" I'd asked for reassurance.

"Yes. I just told you I did."

It wasn't exactly what she'd said, but I was smart enough to drop it at the time.

Either way, I had a hell of a lot to be thankful for this year.

—Zary—

"I want details," Ava said to Aine as she walked over and closed the bedroom door.

I looked between the two.

"I really like him," Aine admitted.

"Who?" I asked.

"Striker. She brought him with her."

"He met me here, but you're right. I invited him."

I nodded. "They're seeing each other."

"Wait," said Ava. "You know already?"

"He's a good man."

Aine shrugged. "He is. Although…"

"What?" asked Ava.

"Gunner doesn't like him."

"That isn't true," I told them. "He respects him. It's just that Gunner struggles with telling people how he feels."

"You really love him," said Ava.

"I do. I have for a very long time. Years, in fact."

"Wait. How?"

I told them about the day I first saw him, and how I'd risked my own life instead of killing him. "If anyone had found out I let him go, I would've been killed."

"What happened next?" asked Aine.

"Nothing. I didn't see him again for a long time, but I always knew he was the man I was meant to be with. I know now that he felt the same way."

"Oh my God. That's so romantic," gushed Ava.

"I'm so glad for you," added Aine. "You and Gunner both deserve to be happy."

"We all do," said Ava. "We all deserve to have men in our lives who love us, make us feel safe, and whom we love just as much."

"And who tell us their real names."

Ava and I laughed.

"I'm serious."

"What is Striker's real name?" asked Ava.

"Griffin Ellis."

"It sounds so…regal."

"I know, right?"

"Regal? Like a king?" I asked.

Ava nodded.

"Yes. I agree."

"This is really nice," murmured Ava.

"Thank you for pushing," I said, smiling. "But now," I threw the covers off. "I have to use the lavatory."

"Me too," said Ava. "Just wait until you're pregnant, Aine. You'll find out that you have to pee all the time."

"Uh, TMI, both of you."

—*Gunner*—

I'd come back down the hallway, but hurried away from the bedroom door so they didn't catch me eavesdropping. Things between Zary and her half-sisters were going better than I'd hoped.

"Whatcha' doin'?" asked Odette, walking in the front door.

"Hey, Sis," I said, kissing her cheek.

Odette pulled back. "Who are you?"

"I know. Sometimes I don't recognize myself."

My sister put her arms around me. "I'm happy for you."

"Yeah, there's a lot of that goin' around."

"I need some of what you've got."

"Things didn't work out with Tim?"

Odette shook her head. "That ended a long time ago."

"Uh…sorry to hear that."

She burst out laughing. "Now you're going overboard."

"I know. You should've seen me a couple of weeks ago when I had to ask Doc about his baby." I shuddered and my sister giggled.

"Pretty soon all you guys will be having conversations about diapers."

"The hell we will," I mumbled while walking back into the kitchen.

7

Ava and Razor

"Where are you hidin' my wife?" I asked, coming into Gunner's kitchen.

"Bathroom."

"Huh?"

"That's where she was headed the last time I saw her," said Gunner.

"Anybody else think this is weird as…oh, hi, Mrs. Godet."

"Razor," she said, kissing my cheek. "Mrs. Godet was my mother-in-law. How many times have I told you to call me Madeline? By the way, where's your mom?"

"Mashing potatoes and adding marshmallows to yams." I cringed. "So gross."

"I'll pop over and see her as soon as I make the stuffing."

"I got this, Ma," said Gunner. "Go be…uh…social."

Madeline stood on her toes and kissed Gunner's cheek. "I'll be back in a minute."

"Hey, man," I said, putting my hand on Striker's shoulder.

"Hey, Razor."

"Just in case no one else has warned you, break Aine's heart or hurt her in any way, and I'll kill you."

Striker laughed; not exactly the reaction I'd expected or wanted.

"I'm not kidding."

"I know you're not, and just to reassure you, Gunner warned me first."

"Good." I moved away from the onions. "You gave him the worst job of all," I said to Gunner. "I like it."

"You're hazing me."

I laughed. "Hi, sweetheart," I said when Ava walked into the kitchen followed by her twin.

"Hi, Tabon," she said, wrapping her arms around my waist.

"Can I help?" I heard Aine ask Striker.

"Nah. I got this."

"I don't mind."

Striker leaned forward and kissed her cheek. "I'm being hazed. Plus if I hurt you in any way, including making you chop onions, they'll both kill me."

"Damn straight," I said. "Back away from the onions, Aine."

"Got a minute?" Ava asked me.

"Got a lifetime of 'em for you, baby." I followed her out of the kitchen and then out the front door. "Where are we going?"

She didn't answer.

"Avarie?"

"We should leave them alone."

"Who?"

"My sister and Striker."

"Why?"

"They don't need an audience."

"Gunner is still there."

"He doesn't hover like you do."

I scrubbed my face with my hand. "Do I really?"

Ava nodded. "I get it. You're protective of Aine, and I love that about you, but she really likes him. It isn't fair of you guys to disparage him in front of her."

I thought she was going too far, using the word disparage, but I'd learned to keep my mouth shut unless it really mattered, and this didn't.

"Got it," I said instead. "No more hovering."

"Thank you, Tabon," she said, kissing my cheek.

"Is that all I get?" I pulled her close and covered her lips with mine. "Give me a real kiss."

—Ava—

God, I loved this man. In my wildest dreams, I never imagined love like our existed. I put my hand on my belly, knowing our child would always feel loved and protected.

Tabon covered my hand with his. "How's my baby?" he asked.

I smiled. "Growing."

"And how's my baby mama?"

"Ew. I hate that term. Your wife is fine."

Tabon laughed. "Sorry, darlin'. How about takin' a walk with me?"

I nodded, and he led me through the trees and out to the beach. "I love it here," I murmured.

"More than Yachats?"

"Nothing compares to home, Tabon, but I do like visiting Cambria. It reminds me of the time right after Quinn and Mercer's wedding."

He scrubbed his face again. "Not great memories, Avarie."

"I disagree. Sure, I'd never choose to go back and live that time of my life over again, but it was when I realized I love you."

"Me too."

"But neither of us said it."

"Wouldn't it have been weird? That soon?"

I told him what Zary had said about the first time she and Gunner met. "Romantic, huh?"

"If you say so."

We walked along quietly, and I loved that we could do that.

"Do you miss going for runs?" he asked.

"I was just thinking that."

"Can you?"

"Run?"

Tabon nodded.

I pulled back from him. "Am I getting that big?"

"No." He laughed and pulled me closer. "No one would even be able to tell that you're pregnant. I just meant, is it safe?"

I shrugged. "I don't know why it wouldn't be."

"We'll try a short one tomorrow."

I scrunched my eyes. "Feeling out of shape?"

Tabon laughed again. "It doesn't matter what kind of shape I'm in, you'll always outrun me."

"You got that right."

—Razor—

When we got back to the house, I saw a car pulling through the gate.

"Who's that?" Ava asked.

"Looks like Mantis."

"I didn't know he was coming."

"Me either. Shit."

"What?"

"Dutch and Alegria are coming too."

"And?"

I told her what I knew about their past.

"Oh. Who invited Mantis?"

I shrugged. "No idea. Maybe Gunner."

"This will be awkward."

"It isn't like we all haven't been in the same place at the same time before. Although…"

"What?"

"I think Dutch was keeping the thing with Alegria a secret."

"Thing?"

"I'm not certain, but I think they're together."

"Why would they keep it a secret?"

I shrugged again and led her over to the place where Mantis had parked. "Let's not say anything," I whispered.

"You're worse than girls," she muttered.

"Hey, Mantis. Welcome. Come on in. When did you get to town?"

"Thanks. I've been here since Monday."

"Why haven't you come by before now?"

Mantis told him about exploring the area. "I was happy for the time alone."

I nodded. "You haven't said much about your last op."

Mantis shook his head and looked at Ava.

"I'll be inside," she said, letting go of my hand.

"You don't have to—"

"It's okay, Mantis. I was heading in to see what I could do to help anyway." She kissed my cheek, and I patted her bottom as she walked away.

"That's my wife," I mumbled. How had I gotten so damn lucky?

"I envy you."

"Yeah? It wasn't that long ago that we were all single and planning to stay that way."

"Being single is fucking overrated."

"Sorry, didn't mean to touch on a sore subject."

"If you're talking about Alegria, that ended before I left for Afghanistan."

"How is she?"

Mantis told me what he knew about the surgery and the doctor's expectations. "She's tough. Maybe even tougher than me." He laughed. "She'll be okay."

It wasn't hard to see that Mantis was still in love with Alegria. If I told him now that she and Dutch were on their way here, would he leave? Probably, and then he'd spend Thanksgiving alone, and that wouldn't be cool.

"Come on in. Can I get you a beer?"

"I'd love one. Thanks."

I introduced Mantis to my mom and to Gunner's mom, who looked like she was doing more chatting than helping, but I doubted my best friend cared all that much. Gunner usually liked to be alone—or at least he used to prefer it that way. Now, like me, he'd probably want to be alone with his woman more than anything.

"I saw Striker the day I got here."

"Yeah? He didn't mention it. Although I doubt he's got much more on his mind other than Aine."

"I noticed that too."

I heard the front door open, and the sound of my two nieces about to barrel into the kitchen.

"Whoa, slow down there."

They stopped to hug me and then looked at Mantis.

"Sierra, Savannah, this is my friend Mr. Cassman. Can you say hello?"

Both girls impatiently shook Mantis' hand.

"Where's Ava?" Sierra asked.

"Hmm. Not sure. Upstairs maybe."

"Uncle Razor," said Savannah with her hands on her hips. "How come you don't know where your *wife* is?"

Both girls broke into a fit of giggles.

"What's so funny?" asked my sister, coming in followed by Monk, who was carrying two pies.

"Hey, Saylor," I said, kissing her cheek. "I've lost Ava." I looked at my nieces. "Why don't you two go find her for me?"

"I'll get the rest," said Monk.

"Need help?" asked Mantis.

Monk nodded.

I chuckled. Why speak when a head movement would suffice?

"I'm getting used to it," said Saylor.

"How quiet Monk is?"

"Yep."

"Wait. How used to it?"

"Don't go there, Raze," she said, winking.

"Jesus. Can't anyone find somebody outside of K19 to get involved with?"

"Some of your partners—one in particular—is pretty damn hot."

"Stop it. Seriously. No talking about anything hot." I put my hands over my ears.

"Where's dinner?" Saylor asked.

"Over here."

"Where?"

I took her into the dining room. "I guess I need to add a few more leaves to the table."

"I'll say. How many in total?"

"Uh, sixteen. I think. Wait, no, it'll be an odd number. No, that's wrong too. Shit. I don't know. Can't we just set up a bunch of tables and everyone can eat where they want?"

Saylor nodded. "Probably a better idea. Why don't you go hang out with your buddies and let the women folk take care of this?"

"If I said something like that, I'd never hear the end of it."

"You got that right. Now git."

"Is Monk from the South?"

"Yeah, why?"

"He must do some talking. I've never, ever heard you say 'git' before."

Saylor smiled. It was nice to see. Her ex-husband had been a first-class asshole.

I leaned in close to my sister. "How is Monk with the girls?"

She put her hand on my arm. "He's great with them, and they love him."

"Isn't it kinda soon?"

"They know he's their mama's special friend. We don't do sleepovers, and we keep the PDA to a minimum."

I'd asked, so I supposed I deserved to get an answer, but I definitely didn't want to hear any more details.

"That's awesome," I said, walking away. "Call if you change your mind and want my help. Actually, text. I'm goin' next door after I find my wife and those two little rascals."

"You like that word, don't you?"

"Rascals? Yep. One of my favorites. It's one of those words that is so perfect. Don't need a thesaurus to find one that's more fitting."

"You're a weirdo. I meant 'wife.'"

I winked and waved. "I know you did."

I found Ava and the girls upstairs. All three were on the bed, and my nieces each had one hand on my wife's belly.

"How big is the baby now?" I heard Sierra ask.

"About this big." Ava held both hands up about four inches apart. "And he or she weighs about an ounce. Do you know how much that is?"

They shook their heads.

"Okay, let me think. What's a good example? I know, the turkey we're having for Thanksgiving dinner probably weights twenty-five pounds. It takes sixteen ounces to make one pound."

"Wow," the girls said in unison. "Cool."

Ava looked up and smiled at me. "There's your Uncle Razor now."

"Don't you mean Uncle Tabon?" asked Savannah.

"Nope. I'm the only one who calls him that, so for you two, he'll always be your Uncle Razor."

"I like Razor better anyway," said Sierra.

Savannah smacked her. "That wasn't nice. How would you like it if someone said they didn't like your name? You should apologize."

Sierra looked and me, and I smiled. "No apology necessary. I used to like Razor better too. Until I met your Aunt Avarie."

Ava blew me a kiss, and my heart melted. I sure had a lot to be thankful for this year.

8

Aine and Striker

I washed my hands and went in search of Aine. I found her sitting on the deck, looking out at the ocean.

"Whatcha' thinkin' about?"

She turned, smiled at me, and her cheeks turned the prettiest shade of pink I'd ever seen. "How nice it is that you're here."

"No place I'd rather be."

"Not missing your family?"

"No. My family…"

"You haven't said much about them."

I sat down next to her and pulled her over to my lap. "As you well know, families come with good and bad. I didn't get much good."

"I'm sorry. I shouldn't have—"

I interrupted her apology with a kiss, and then rested my forehead against hers. "Like I said, there's no place I'd rather be."

"Me too."

"By the way, where's your mom?"

"Still at the inn. Peggy doesn't cook."

I laughed. "Enough said. I think there are too many cooks in those kitchens anyway."

"I'm not a great cook either."

"I bet you just say that. I remember some pretty good peanut butter and jelly sandwiches. You're probably a great cook."

Aine laughed. "I think you made them. And, no, I'm terrible. Ava will attest that I should never be allowed in a kitchen. I just offered to help chop the onions to be nice." Her cheeks turned pink again.

"You don't have any idea how pretty you are, do you?"

She put her head on my shoulder. "Thank you," she murmured.

"Aine, I…"

When I didn't continue, she looked up at me. "What?"

"Never mind. I forgot what I was going to say."

She nodded. "You're lying, but that's okay."

I laughed. "I'm just really happy to be here with you. I feel like I've said it too many times."

"You never have to apologize for saying you're happy to be with me, Griffin."

"I need to ask you something, though."

Her eyes were still focused on mine. "Okay."

"We really haven't talked about it, and we should have, before now, before I got here earlier in the week."

"Are you about to tell me that your real name isn't Griffin Ellis?"

"No. Why would you think that?"

Aine laughed. "Earlier when Ava and I were talking to Zary, Ava said all three of us deserve to be happy. We deserve to feel loved and safe. And I added that we deserve to be with men who tell us their real names. I was kidding. Sort of. I mean, my dad…"

"I get it and I agree. You deserve to be happy."

"What did you want to talk about?"

I moved her from my lap back to the chair she'd been sitting in.

"You're worrying me," she murmured.

"I'm sorry. It's just that…I'm a lot older than you are, Aine."

"Oh. Well…um…okay."

I leaned forward and took her hands in mine. "This isn't about you. You're perfect. I just want to be sure you realize I'm a few years older than Razor." Aine looked like she was going to cry. Damn, I was making a mess of this.

"Does it matter? I mean, am I too…inexperienced for you?"

"God, no. It's more that I started wondering if you knew. And if you didn't, if it would bother you."

"I like you, Griffin. I don't care how old you are. It isn't something I've given any thought to because, to me, all that matters is that we enjoy being together."

"I just want you to know, if you change your mind, I'll understand."

She was quiet long enough that I began to feel uncomfortable. Plus, she wasn't looking at me; she was looking out at the ocean again.

"I wish you'd tell me what you're thinking."

"I wish you wouldn't let me go so easily."

"I just want to be sure you're sure. Does that make any sense?"

Aine stood and walked into the house, but I didn't follow. Somehow our conversation had gone from bad to worse, and I had no idea what to do about it.

—Aine—

I left Gunner's and walked next door. "Is Ava over here?" I asked.

"I think she's upstairs," said Razor's mother.

I took the stairs two at a time, hoping I'd get up them quickly enough that no one would see me crying.

"Ava?" I said when I got to the bedroom door. "Are you in there?"

The door opened a few seconds later, and two young girls came bounding out.

"Hi," they said in unison. "You're Aunt Ava's sister."

I wiped my tears and bent down. "I am. How are you?"

"We're fine. Anyway, bye," the older of the two said.

Off they went, running down the stairs I'd just come up. I crossed the room and lay on the bed, next to my sister.

"What's wrong?"

"I just had the weirdest conversation with Griffin."

"Tell me what he said."

"He wanted me to know that he's a lot older than I am."

"Okay, so…why?"

"I don't know. I told him it didn't bother me, and then he said that if I changed my mind, he'd understand."

"Hmm. That's weird."

"That's what I thought. Do you think he's trying to dump me?"

"No. Definitely not. It's gotta be something he's worried about, even if you're not. What else did he say?"

"Not much."

"What did you say?"

"That I wished he wouldn't let me go so easily."

Ava was thoughtful for a minute. "It's his problem, Aine. It isn't about you. Maybe someone dumped him in the past because of it."

I shrugged. "I don't know. It kind of seemed like he was giving me an out."

"When is he supposed to leave?"

"We were talking about leaving tomorrow and driving up the coast."

"To where?"

"Yachats."

"Wow. That sounds nice. I say, see how that goes. If it's weird, then you know."

"Here are my girls," said our mom, coming in the bedroom door. "What are you talking about?"

"Striker told Aine he thinks he's too old for her."

"*Ava!*" I swatted her. "That isn't what he said."

"Men." Our mother shook her head. "You never know what's going to set them off. I mean, look at Paul. He finds out my ex-husband is a Russian mobster, and he asks for a divorce."

"Right." I didn't think what Griffin said had anything to do with our mom's soon-to-be ex-husband, but that's how Peggy was. How do you give counsel to a daughter you never spent any time with? At least she wasn't drinking anymore. Or it didn't seem like she was.

"Thanks, Mom," I said and got off the bed.

"Oh. I came to tell you we'll be eating in forty-five minutes."

I helped my sister off the bed too, and we followed our mother down the stairs.

"Where's Striker?" Ava asked.

Razor stepped closer to us. "He went to pick up Dutch and Alegria from the train station. He said to let you know he'll be back in thirty."

"Why are you whispering?" I asked.

He motioned with his head toward Mantis, who was standing on the other side of the room.

"He doesn't know they're coming."

"Oh. I'm lost, but that's okay. I've got enough drama of my own."

Razor's head snapped up. "What did Striker do?"

I patted his arm. "Nothing. He's just worried that he's too old for me."

"Oh. Well…he is."

Ava and I laughed when Razor walked away.

—Striker—

"Thanks for the lift," said Dutch, opening the car door for Alegria.

"No problem. Although I didn't realize how tight the back seat was."

"Not a problem," said Dutch, folding himself into a space made for someone a quarter of his size.

"How are you doing?" I asked Alegria when she sat in the front.

"Okay. The pain meds should kick in soon."

"Taking the train wasn't the best idea. We should've just driven," Dutch said from where he sat sideways in the back.

These two looked as miserable as I felt after my conversation with Aine.

"The house isn't too far from here."

"We've been there," Alegria said to me. Snapped at me was more accurate.

"Alegria," Dutch murmured from the back.

I looked over, unable to read anything but tension on her face. Despite the fact we'd been on many missions together, I didn't know the woman that well.

She, Dutch, and Mantis were all former Air Force officers, a branch of the military that got plenty of ribbing for being the pampered set.

The truth was, Alegria and Mantis had flown sorties resulting in the deaths of some of the worst terrorists in the world, and those missions hadn't been danger-free.

I had a hell of a lot of respect for the men and women who flew any kind of fighter jet, regardless of military branch.

Onyx, the only other pilot on the K19 team, had served in the Marine Corps like most of the partners had, flying F/A 18 Hornets. While those planes were being replaced by the Lightning II, F-35 Joint Strike Fighter, the Hornets had long provided fighter escort, enemy defenses suppression, air control, reconnaissance, and close air support of Marines on the ground.

K19 was mighty lucky to have all three of them on our team.

The drive back to Cambria was quiet since neither Alegria nor Dutch seemed to be in the mood to talk. I didn't mind, though. It gave me time to think about what I'd said to Aine.

I'd wanted her to be aware of my age, given I was fifteen years her senior. That was it. If she ever decided she didn't want to spend her time with an old fart, I wanted her to know that I'd understand. That had somehow turned into her asking if she was too inexperienced for me.

Our first night together had been magical as far as I was concerned. That she would think it was anything less than that, baffled me.

***

We were seated at the table in the front window of the Sea Chest, so we could look out at the moon's light on the ocean while we ate.

"This place is fantastic," I said between bites of the freshest halibut I'd ever eaten.

"I agree, but I'm so full I can't finish."

We'd started out with a dozen oysters, followed by clam chowder, sourdough bread, and our entrées.

Aine ordered a calamari steak served abalone-style, which I was all too happy to finish for her.

"Cheers," I said, toasting her with a twenty-year tawny port. "Here's to many more dinners shared by the light of the moon."

Aine looked out at the ocean; something she did a lot, I'd noticed. "Tell me what's on your mind."

She looked back at me. "I'm not sure how to say this."

"We've talked for hours, pretty girl. Just say it."

"I haven't been with very many men," she said almost too quietly for me to hear her.

I leaned forward, grasped her neck, and kissed her. "Whatever has or hasn't happened in either of our pasts, doesn't matter, Aine. This is just me and you. Okay?"

I draped my arm around her shoulders on our walk back to the inn. Every once in a while, I'd stop and hold her close while I brushed her lips with mine, and then kissed her the way I'd wished I could every time we'd talked on the phone.

"Here you are, in my arms," I said when we got back to the inn. "Do you know how many nights I've wished we were holding each other just like this?"

"It's been the same for me. I fall asleep imagining your arms are around me."

***

"Wasn't that the turn?" Alegria asked, pointing at the road I'd just driven past.

I'd been so lost in thought, remembering the first night Aine and I were together, I might've driven all the way to San Simeon before I realized it.

I took the next left turn, which also went to Moonstone Beach Road.

"Sorry," I murmured, but I wasn't. Being away from the house had given me time to think, and I'd come to a decision. Aine McNamara was my dream come true, and I'd heard what she said earlier: *I wish you wouldn't let me go so easily.*

If that's the way she felt, then I would wrestle the devil himself to keep her in my life.

Instead of worrying about whether Aine thought I was too old for her, I was going to appreciate every minute we could spend together.

I had a hell of a lot to be thankful for this year, and she was at the top of the list. It was time I let her know that, instead of giving her an out she hadn't asked for.

—Aine—

"Is there anything else I can do to help?" Mantis asked.

"I think we've got everything. As soon as Razor and Gunner finish carving the turkeys, we'll be set," said Gunner's mother.

"Griffin isn't back yet," I murmured, carrying a bowl of mashed potatoes out to the table that had been set up as a buffet.

"He just pulled through the gate," said Razor.

I set the potatoes down and hurried out the front door. I hated the way I'd walked away from him before he left, and I wanted him to know how sorry I was.

I bit my bottom lip as I watched him get out of the car and stalk straight to me.

"Come with me," he said, taking my hand. When we got around the side of the house, Griffin pushed me up against one of the big redwood trees. "Listen to me," he said, his lips so close to mine, I could feel his breath. "I'm not letting you go. Easily or otherwise. I want you in my life, Aine, more than I've ever wanted anyone. Do you understand?"

I nodded.

"Not just in my bed. In my *life*."

"I want that too, Griffin. I'm sorry I walked away from you."

"Don't do it again. Don't ever walk away from me. Stay and talk it out. Tell me what you're thinking, and I'll do the same. If you aren't sure what I mean, ask me."

"I will. I promise."

He held my face with his hand and kissed me hard.

"We're waiting on you two," we heard someone yell.

"Go ahead without us," Griffin yelled back.

I giggled. "We should go in."

"You're right. The faster we eat, the faster we can be alone again."

"I'm not that hungry, so it won't take me long," I confessed.

"Me neither. Not for Thanksgiving dinner, that is."

9

Mantis, Alegria, and Dutch

"You should've told me," I said to Razor when Alegria and Dutch walked in the front door.

"They didn't know you'd be here either," he answered, although I already guessed as much based on the look on both of their faces.

Dutch walked straight over to me, while Alegria was waylaid by the group gathering around her at the front door.

"Connecticut?"

"Whatever." I walked away, but Dutch followed.

"She isn't doing very well."

"Then, you should take better care of her."

Dutch scrubbed his face with his hand. "She needs you."

I was livid, more because Dutch was pulling this shit in a room full of people than from what he was saying. Granted, no one could hear us, but if I did what

I wanted to do and slammed my fist into Dutch's face, all eyes would be on us.

"You don't think I knew you wanted her? Now you've got her. Be thankful and leave me the hell alone."

When I went to get a plate, Dutch didn't follow, and for that, I was thankful.

The man, or men, I was pissed at more than anyone else were Razor and Gunner, but I got it. If they'd told me Dutch and Alegria were coming, I would've left, and they both knew it.

"We'd like to propose a toast," said Razor, holding up his glass. "If we could have your attention for a minute."

"We should've waited until everyone was eating and was quiet," said Gunner, raising his glass too.

"Yeah, well, they aren't eating until we make this toast, so they better pipe down."

Once everyone stopped talking, Razor looked around the room. "Everyone got a drink? If not, my beautiful, smart, gracious wife and her equally amazing twin will bring you one."

I stepped forward and took a glass of red wine. I swirled and sniffed, recognizing the Burgundy right away. The *Tollot-Beaut* from *Chorey-lès-Beaune* was one of my favorites. Manon's too. In fact, I'd bet she'd recommended it.

The anger I'd felt at Dutch seemed to fade away when her eyes met mine from across the room. I raised my glass. "To you," I mouthed, took a drink, and then turned back toward Razor.

"Everyone ready?"

The group collectively responded with murmurs of assent.

"First of all, I want to thank all of you for being here with us today, and to Alegria, for having a case of this fabulous wine delivered yesterday."

All eyes turned to her, including mine.

"*À votre santé,*" Gunner toasted, but I hardly heard it above everything Manon's eyes were saying to me. Longing and love—I recognized both. She didn't blink as she took a drink at the same time I did.

When Dutch approached and put his arm around her shoulders, the spell was broken. I turned away from them both and took another drink.

I would allow myself one glass. No more than that, for once dinner was over, I'd find my hosts, thank them, and leave. In the meantime, I intended to stay as far away from Alegria and Dutch as I could.

"Mind if I join you?" I asked Striker and Aine, who were seated outside on the deck, at a table with only one open seat.

"Please," answered Aine. "Have you met my mother?"

"I haven't. Gehring Cassman, but most people here call me Mantis."

"What a fascinating nickname. How did you get it?"

"His freakishly abnormal stereoscopic vision," said Striker between forkfuls of turkey and stuffing. "It's his call sign. Mantis is a pilot."

"Actually, I was given the name due to my supernatural powers."

Striker laughed. "You keep telling yourself that."

I heard a familiar ringtone and watched as Striker stood and pulled his phone from his pocket.

"Excuse me," he said, his playful demeanor abruptly changing.

Striker was far enough away that no one could hear what he was saying, but I knew what the tone meant. Soon he'd return to the table and tell me where he needed to go and how quickly he needed to get there. As the only pilot here, other than Alegria, who wouldn't be flying again anytime soon, I'd take the assignment without question or hesitation. It's what I would've done if I were one of twenty pilots here.

"Aine, can I speak to you privately?" Striker said when he returned to the table. He turned to me. "Mantis, stand by."

"Roger that."

I finished the food on my plate, took it inside, and dumped the rest of the wine in my glass.

"What's going on?" asked Alegria.

I hadn't seen her follow me into the kitchen.

"I'm afraid Mantis and I have to cut our visit short," answered Striker, coming back inside with Aine.

"Where are you going?" she asked.

"Alegria," admonished Striker, looking directly at Aine and her mother, who had just walked into the room.

"I'll just say my goodbyes. Fifteen minutes?" I said to Striker.

"Roger that."

"Wait." I felt Alegria's hand on my arm. I closed my eyes, wishing I didn't have to have this conversation.

"Where are you going?" she asked again.

"I don't know."

"And you agreed to the op anyway."

"Look around you. Who else is there, Alegria?"

"It wouldn't matter if there were five other pilots here," she said, echoing the thoughts I'd just had.

"Let it be," I said, softening my voice. "It was nice to see you today."

When she unexpectedly threw her arms around me, I took a deep breath and rested my head against the side of hers.

"Be safe," she whispered.

"Always, *mon coeur.*" The words were rote, but that didn't diminish their meaning. She'd been my heart for most of my life. Whether we were together or not, wouldn't change that. Maybe one day another woman would take her place, but I didn't see that happening any time soon.

—Dutch—

I stood to the side and watched the two people who mattered more to me than any others, wishing things were the way they used to be between us.

Mantis walked away from Alegria and straight over to me.

"Shipping out. I'll be in touch."

"Be safe," I said, reaching out to shake his hand.

"What's that shit?" Mantis said, pulling me into a hug.

"I didn't know—"

"You always *know.*"

I felt like a bigger asshole than I had a few minutes ago. We'd never let each other leave without a proper send-off.

"Godspeed," I said, squeezing Mantis' shoulder.

"Appreciate it."

I looked into Alegria's eyes when Mantis walked away. They were filled with so much sadness, it nearly shredded my heart. She was like a bird with a broken wing, powerless to do the thing she was best at—fly.

It wouldn't be long before she mended, and when she did, would the time come when she finally admitted she wanted Mantis more than she wanted me?

—*Alegria*—

My own stubborn pride put me where I was, and would keep me there if I didn't let it go and tell Mantis I forgave him.

Was that even fair? Was choosing to live by the commitment he'd made to serve his country something he should be forgiven for?

I'd wanted him to choose me, and he didn't, and that's the part I hadn't been able to forgive—until the day in the hospital when I woke up and he was there.

From that moment on, I'd been questioning the decision I made to end things with Mantis. No matter how strongly I denied the things Dutch said about me still loving Mantis, was he wrong?

I wasn't being any more fair to Dutch than I had been to Mantis when I gave him the ultimatum. Dutch loved me, and all he wanted in return was for me to love him back. I did, but not in the way he wanted. There was only one man I loved the way Dutch wanted me to love him—Mantis. Could what I felt for Dutch be enough for him, or would the time come when he walked away from me too?

—Mantis—

"Where are we going?"

Striker sighed. "I won't know for sure until I receive the briefing."

"Not the final destination, Striker. I need to know where we're going now. I can't submit a flight plan unless I know where I'm taking you."

"Right. Sorry. McLean."

I nodded. "Headquarters."

"We had plans."

"What's that?"

"Aine and I. I was supposed to spend the rest of the week with her. I rented this car for our drive up the coast. I was taking her back to Yachats."

"Sorry, man."

"I thought that once I quit working for the company, I'd be able to choose." Striker looked over at me when I didn't respond. "No comment?"

"It's never been a choice for me, Striker."

"Elaborate."

"That's what ended Alegria and me. She thought I had a choice."

—Alegria—

"We need to talk."

"Dutch, I'm exhausted and I want to sleep."

"I know, but if I don't do this now, I'm afraid I won't do it at all."

I sighed and folded my arms. "What is it?"

"I saw what happened with Mantis."

"What's your point?"

"Why can't you admit that you're still in love with him?"

"I can't do this now. What's more? I won't. I'm tired. I'm in pain, and I have no intention of discussing it with you."

"What if you have no choice?" he asked.

"I always have a choice," I answered.

10

Zary and Gunner

"I need your help," I said to Ava when she answered my call.

"With what?" Ava responded in her usual cheery way. Did nothing ever bother my half-sister?

"It's almost Christmas and I don't have a gift for Gunner."

"Oh. Okay. Um. Do you have any ideas?"

"None." I felt like crying.

"Give me a minute. I'll call you back."

Ava hung up before I could tell her we were at Gunner's mother's house and that, while he'd gone downstairs, I expected him back at any minute. Fortunately, my phone rang less than a minute later.

Tabon and I can bring the gifts with us next week, but don't worry, I'll take photos for you so you know what they are. I'll also wrap everything."

"Wait. You'll wrap *everything?* What does that mean?"

"Well, you want to get him one or two bigger gifts, and then a few smaller things too. Have you hung stockings yet?"

I rubbed my temples. "This is so complicated," I muttered, not intending to say it out loud. "I don't know what that means."

"What decorating have you done?"

"We aren't on the island."

"You aren't? Why not? Never mind, it doesn't matter. This is perfect, though. Aine and I will pick you up in an hour, and we'll take you shopping. Tell Gunner you'll be gone most of the afternoon."

"But I only need one gift."

"Trust me on this. You want to get more than that."

"Why?"

"You'll see."

I disconnected the call and went in search of Gunner. I found him downstairs, sitting in front of a computer while he talked on the phone.

"I said today," I heard him bark at whoever was on the other end. "Not tomorrow, not the day after. *Today.* Do whatever you have to, to make that happen."

He slammed his phone down on the desk hard enough that I wondered if he'd shattered the screen.

I turned to walk away before he noticed me but ran into Odette coming down the stairs.

"Hey, Zary. Have you seen Gunner?"

When I turned to point, Gunner was standing in the doorway.

"How much of that did you hear?" he asked.

I cringed. "Just the last thing you said."

He walked over and put his arm around my waist. "I'm sorry."

"For what?"

"I just wish…"

"What?"

"I don't want your surprise to be ruined."

I shook my head. "Then, you should stop talking because I don't know anything other than that you're angry with someone."

"I love you," he murmured, pulling me close and kissing my forehead.

"I love you too. I came to tell you I'm going out."

Gunner raised his brow and smiled. "You are?"

"Yes. Ava and Aine will pick me up in an hour."

"I like it."

I folded my arms.

"Don't give me that look. All I'm saying is that I like that you're spending time with Ava and Aine."

"Why?"

Gunner leaned in closer. "You have a family, Rocket Girl. People who love and care about you. None of us can have too much love in our lives." He rested his hand on my belly. "And this little one will have two grandmothers, three aunts, and lots of honorary uncles in his or her life. That isn't a bad thing."

I nodded. What he said was true, but something inside of me was having a hard time trusting it was real, and if it was, that it would last.

"Can I come along?" Odette asked. "I still have a few things to pick up."

"I guess so." Would that be okay with Ava? I had no idea.

Odette smiled. "I'm sure they won't mind."

"Give me a kiss before you leave," said Gunner.

"And that will be my cue to wait for you upstairs."

Gunner gave me a chaste kiss, and then cupped my face with his hand. "Tell me what's bothering you."

I bit my bottom lip. "I don't know what to give you for Christmas. Am I supposed to get gifts for other people too?" I felt myself getting emotional.

"I'm sure between Ava, Aine, and my sister, they'll help you figure it out. What else is on your mind?"

"Why do you think there's anything else?"

Gunner gazed into my eyes. "Because I know you."

I sighed. There was no point in lying. "There are two things."

Gunner moved his hands to my shoulders and squeezed. "Just tell me."

"Topor."

—*Gunner*—

"Ah, yes. Your uncle."

Zary's mother had hoped her half-brother would be able to join us for the Thanksgiving holiday. He'd said he'd come the day after, but he hadn't shown up. Now he was promising to come to the island, where we were celebrating Christmas.

"Are you worried he will show up, or won't?"

"Both."

"I understand."

"You do?"

I smiled. "You don't want your mother to be disappointed again, but you aren't certain how comfortable you'll feel with a man who first abducted you, and then made you believe he hated you by the way he treated you."

"I don't like that he's coming to the island."

"You don't trust him."

She shook her head. "Not at all."

"What's the second thing?"

"I got a call earlier."

"From?"

"Losha."

"And? Has she finally accepted that United Russia is no longer a threat and is ready to come above ground?"

The last I'd heard, Shiver still hadn't found where she was hiding, let alone convince her that he and the K19 team had successfully negotiated the removal of the bounty UR had placed on her head.

Zary bit her lip. "Not exactly. She…"

When Zary tried to turn away from me, I held her close and looked into her eyes. "You can trust me, sweetheart. No matter what it is."

"Can you look inside my mind? How do you do that?"

"Lifetimes of loving you."

She smiled, and even though it was tentative, it warmed my heart.

"What I'm about to tell you…you can't tell anyone. You have to promise me."

I held up one hand. "I swear I won't tell a soul."

"She's here."

I did my best not to react. Now I understood her insistence that I not tell anyone. By anyone, she meant Shiver. "Where?"

"Washington, and she needs a place to stay. Somewhere…private."

"I see."

The solution was simple, but before I made any promises, I needed to talk to my mother.

"I may have an idea for both Topor and Losha."

"What?"

"I'll tell you when you get back from shopping. Will she be okay wherever she is until then?"

Zary nodded. "Thank you," she murmured.

"Wait," I said when she turned to go up the stairs.

"What?"

"Kiss me."

Zary smiled again, making the hallway, along with my life, brighter.

"I love you."

"You told me that a few minutes ago."

I gripped her arm, pulled her close, and covered her mouth with mine. I leaned into her, pushing her up against the wall, while my tongue invaded her mouth.

"Any questions?" I asked, pulling back so I could see her eyes.

"I love you, Gunner."

"That's better. Have fun today. Oh, wait. I have something for you."

"Oh no, is it a gift? I don't have anything for you."

I walked back over to where my laptop was and pulled an envelope out of my bag.

"What is this?" she asked, pulling out a letter with a credit card attached.

"What does it look like? It's a credit card. Actually, it's a debit card, but it can be used either way. I added you to my account."

Zary hadn't talked to me about it, but Striker told me that United Russia had managed to empty her bank accounts when they knew her intention was to defect. She had money, but it wouldn't last forever, and I didn't want her to be worried about it.

"Gunner, I—"

I closed her hand around the card, leaned forward, and kissed her again. "Don't argue, Rocket Girl. What's mine is yours."

"But…"

"Go ahead. Say whatever it is."

"Thank you."

"Hmm. I know there's something else you were going to say, but I'll accept your thanks. You're welcome."

I went upstairs after I knew Zary and my sister were gone.

"Hello, handsome," my mother said when I walked into the kitchen.

I smiled. "You're in a good mood." She wasn't always, not since my father died.

"You're spending Christmas with me, and I have a grandbaby on the way."

"About Christmas…"

She put her hands on her hips.

"I was just thinking it might be better if we celebrated here rather than on the island."

"I have to admit when you told me your plan, I thought it was awfully ambitious."

"That means people would be coming here. We can keep it simple, though."

"It won't be any different than when your father used to invite half his unit over. In fact, your group is smaller." She wiped her hands on a dish towel. "This means we'll have to get busy. When will your sister and Zary be back?"

"I don't know, and why do we have to get busy? I just said we can keep it simple."

"*Gunner.*" My mother laughed. "We aren't having a houseful of people over for Christmas and not decorate."

I looked around the main floor of the house. It looked plenty decorated to me. "What else is there to do?"

"You run up and bring the rest of the Christmas boxes down from the attic. We can finish everything but the tree. I think Zary might enjoy going with us to pick one out, don't you?"

I shook my head and started for the stairs. It was no use arguing with her about it. If I didn't help, she'd do it on her own.

"Wait. Before you go, tell me who all is coming."

"Same group as Thanksgiving, although I haven't heard whether Striker or Mantis will be able to make it."

"With Svetlana staying here, that leaves five bedrooms. Let's have Razor, Ava, and Sally stay here in the main house. Plus Aine and Peggy. Oh, and Saylor, and the girls. We'll put Savannah and Sierra in the den. I'm assuming Monk will be coming too."

"They have rooms already at the Annapolis Inn."

"They'll be checking out before the end of the week."

"I'm sure they'll be able to tack a few extra days on."

I remembered the look my mother was giving me from when I was a child. It always meant that whatever I'd said was preposterous.

"I guess that look means they won't be able to."

My mother shook her head. "Who does that leave? Just Dutch and Alegria? They can stay in the guest house with Odette. There will be plenty of room if Mantis is able to join us, and of course, Striker and Aine can always stay at his place in McLean and drive in if he makes it back before Christmas. They'll probably want the privacy."

My mother really wasn't talking to me; it was more that she was thinking out loud as she scribbled notes on a piece of paper.

"Am I forgetting anyone?" she asked.

"First of all, how did you remember that much? How did you know it in the first place?"

"Oh, Gunner, how do you think?"

"*Jesus.* Will you quit with that look? I'm not ten years old, and I don't have any idea. That's why I asked."

She patted my arm. "Sally and I talk almost every morning—"

"You talk to Razor's mother every day?"

She patted my arm again. "Yes, but I wasn't finished, sweetheart. I also talk to Peggy, and Svetlana and I are doing quite well with that translation thing you put on my phone. Although her English is coming along so well, I'm not sure how much longer we'll even need it."

I shook my head.

"This is far more practical, Gunner. I'm glad you changed your mind about trying to ferry everyone to the island. Not to mention, the house there really isn't suitable for a group this large."

"I didn't plan for everyone to sleep there," I mumbled.

"It'll be so much nicer this way, and we certainly have the room."

After my father retired and we settled back in Annapolis, he'd built this house on the ten-acre property he'd inherited from his parents. The original dwelling sat farther back from the bay and was about a quarter of the size of the one we were standing in. Once construction finished on the new one, he'd turned the old one into a guest house.

At the time, I'd wondered why my parents needed a house with eight bedrooms plus three more in the original house, but I didn't questioned it. My father had worked hard his whole life, as had my mother. She deserved to live wherever and however she wanted after moving more than fifteen times in the course of my dad's career.

I walked out to the screened porch that overlooked the outdoor kitchen, pool, spa, tennis courts, and the deep-water slip where my beloved Hinckley Bermuda 40, *Whiskey Tango Foxtrot,* usually sat. It had been too long since I'd had time to sail her. Maybe in the spring, Zary and I would join the yacht club and sail in the summer race series.

"There will come a time you'll regret that name, Son," my father had said when I first pulled her into the slip.

"Nah. It's a great name."

My father had laughed. "For a single guy like you, sure, but once you have a family and my grandchildren start asking what the name means, I'll tell them to ask their father."

I remembered wondering if I'd ever have children that would need explaining to. At the time, I doubted it very much.

"Ahem," I heard my mother say. "Boxes?"

"On it, Ma."

—Zary—

I'd never felt so tired, even when I'd gone more than forty-eight hours without sleep on one of my assignments.

It was a good thing the vehicle Ava and Aine had picked Odette and me up in was an oversized SUV;

otherwise, there wouldn't have been anywhere to put all the packages.

I still had to pick out gifts for the three women I was with today, but once I got in the swing of Christmas shopping, they'd given me plenty of unintentional hints about what they might like.

"I know you're tired. I am too," said Ava, sitting next to me in the back seat while Aine drove. "But did you have fun?"

I laughed. "Honestly?"

"Uh-oh," said Odette from the front passenger seat.

"No, it's the opposite. It was magical."

Ava squeezed my hand. "I'm so happy," she whispered.

It had also taken me some time to get used to how much money I was spending. A couple of times, I'd considered calling Gunner to make sure I wasn't over-doing it, but Odette had reassured me.

"You looked like you had sticker shock in the last store," she'd said as we were on our way into another.

"I've spent so much money," I'd whispered.

"Oh, girl, you haven't seen anything yet."

"What about your mother?" Ava asked. "Did you see anything for her?"

"I saw too much. I couldn't decide."

"We can always go back out tomorrow before the wrapping party."

Ava and Aine had invited me over to their suite to wrap everything I'd purchased today. I had no idea what to expect, but since I'd had so much fun today, I decided not to stress over it.

I looked out at the snow softly falling outside the SUV's window, and thought about the conversation my mother and I had had two days ago.

***

"Devochka moya," my mother began. *"Nam nuzhno pogovorit'."*

I sat down and held her hands. "We don't have to talk, not if it is too painful," I answered in our native language, Azeri.

"You need to know."

"They told me you and father were dead. They took me to an orphanage."

My mother looked away. "They told me you were dead too. Both of you."

She went on to explain that, at first, she'd stayed at the compound in the Old City until Rauf had come to get her to take her back to Armenia.

"I didn't want to be alive. I tried to take my life," she confessed. "They put me in a hospital for the insane."

"How long were you there?"

"Many, many years. It was almost as though I had died like I'd wanted to. Only Rauf came to see me, and that wasn't often. I expected to live there for the rest of my life."

"How did you get to Baku?"

"Rauf was the one who came to get me from there. I asked where he was taking me, and he told me we had to return to the Old City. When I asked why, he said your father's name."

"And you were held prisoner there?" I asked.

"I had only been there two days before you were rescued. When Rauf told me you were alive, that we had been so close yet not seen each other, I felt my heart break all over again."

"Did you see Petrov?"

"Just once. He told me that Topor, what he called Rauf, had told him I'd gone insane. He said that he'd paid for my care all those years and it was time I paid him back."

"How?"

"He warned me to do what he said, but until the night in the forest…" My mother sobs were heart wrenching.

"No more, Mama. We'll never speak of Petrov again. We're both alive, and I'll take care of you forever."

***

I still hadn't talked to Gunner about our conversation, except to mention Topor and the call from Losha, which really had nothing to do with my mother. Regardless, we needed to talk about it, and whether he'd come up with a place for Losha to stay. I hoped he wouldn't suggest she come to the island with us, because I knew my friend would never agree to it.

—Gunner—

"If anyone had said, 'next year you and Gunner will be decorating the house for Christmas,' I never would've believed them."

"I would've been right there with you, Ma."

"Can I ask you something?"

"You can ask." It was a rote response in our house; both my father and I had said it so often.

"Are you and Zary going to get married?"

"I hope so, Ma. More than anything."

"There she is now," my mother said, looking out the window.

I greeted her at the front door.

"What's all this?" Zary asked, motioning toward the boxes strewn about the living room.

"We're going to spend Christmas here instead of on the island."

Zary's eyes met mine. "Are you sure?"

"I don't think my mother would have it any other way."

"He's right," she said, walking over to hug Zary. "How was shopping?"

"It was fun but…"

"You look exhausted," I murmured, rubbing her back.

"We can finish this up later. Go on now." My mother nudged me toward the stairs.

—Zary—

"I told you I had a solution for both Topor and Losha," Gunner began when we were upstairs, with the bedroom door closed. "Having Christmas here means you won't be stuck on an island with a man you aren't sure you can trust."

I nodded. "I don't think Losha will feel comfortable coming here, Gunner."

"I figured as much. What about the island? Do you think she'd be comfortable there?"

I didn't see why not if she was going to be alone. "Actually, I think it would be perfect. But Gunner—"

"No one will know, Zary. I'll take her there myself."

"Before you do that, there's something else you need to know."

"Go ahead." Gunner waited while I tried to figure out how to tell him something I wasn't sure of myself.

"She might not be alone."

11

Ava and Razor

"How was shopping? *Whoa,* what's all this?" I asked when I opened the back of the SUV.

"Most of it is Zary's, but I bought a few things, and so did Aine."

I unloaded the packages onto a luggage cart. "Gunner called while you were out. He said we're going to spend Christmas at his mother's house instead of on the island."

"Did he say why?"

"Space. His mother's place is a lot bigger. In fact, this will be our last night here. We'll move over there tomorrow. Which bears the question, why did you bring all of Zary's purchases here anyway?"

"To wrap it all tomorrow. She was going to come here—"

"Slow down, Avarie," I said, pulling her into a hug. "We have this room reserved for another three nights. I just thought you might want to spend the extra time with Zary."

"Is his mother sure about us staying there?"

"Wait until you see this place. Oh, and your mom and my mom are already there. I guess I should've told you that first."

"We did see it," said Aine. "When we dropped Zary and Odette off. We just didn't go inside."

"Then, you know it's like a luxury hotel."

"If you're sure…"

"Positive. It'll be great. You two head to the suite. I'll have the bellman help me bring the sleigh full of presents up there."

—Ava—

"Are you okay?" I asked my sister.

"I'll be fine. It isn't like I've ever had a boyfriend at Christmas. This year is just like all the others."

"You still have a boyfriend; he just can't spend Christmas with you."

"Do I? I don't even know at this point."

I knew Aine was heartbroken that she hadn't heard anything from Striker since Thanksgiving. When I'd asked Tabon about it, all he said was that wherever he was, he was in deep.

"Can you ask Doc?"

"I did, sweetheart," he'd said. "There's nothing I can tell you."

That meant he knew, but I shouldn't ask any more questions.

"I wish I could wave a magic wand and get him here, sweetie," I told Aine.

"Me too. But, Ava, can we stop talking about it?"

"Of course." I looked at my phone and saw that Odette was calling. "Hi."

"Change of plans. Did you unload the car yet?"

"Tabon is doing that right now."

"Stop him. You're coming here tonight. We'll just put everything in the guest house."

"He said we were going to stay here one more night."

"Gunner just told me to tell you that he's calling Razor now."

I hung up and went to look for my sister. I found her in the suite's second bedroom, crying, and lay down next to her.

"I wish I had something I could say that would make you feel better."

"I'm just feeling sorry for myself."

"I'll be right back," I said when I heard a knock at the door. I hoped Tabon didn't get all the way up here with the packages already.

"We're here!" screamed Tara and Penelope when I opened the door.

"Oh my gosh. Wow! What are you doing here? Wait. I mean, I'm so glad you're here."

Aine came out of the bedroom and ran up to hug our friends. "I'm so happy to see you both."

"Come in." I moved aside and waved them into the suite.

"How long are you staying?" Aine asked, noticing their bags like I had.

"We're here for Christmas! Didn't—"

"Surprise!" said Tabon, walking in behind them and over to me. "I thought they might help cheer up Aine," he whispered.

"I love you so much," I said, wrapping my arms around his neck.

"Are they like this all the time?" I heard Penelope say to Aine, but I didn't hear my sister's response.

"I'm going to head over to the house and give you ladies some time alone," Tabon said before kissing my cheek.

"I don't know how to thank you for doing this," I said, kissing him back.

"I have a few ideas." Tabon looked over at my sister and our friends. "We'll talk about it later."

"Oh. What about…I mean, where will they stay?"

"Headed there to figure it out. Worst case, they'll stay here."

—*Razor*—

I was on my way down to the SUV when my phone rang. I looked at the screen and saw Doc was calling.

"Tell me you're calling with good news."

"The opposite, I'm afraid. Still no word."

"Shit. This is bad."

"I agree."

"Can we go in and look?"

"That's one of the reasons I'm calling. We need to put a team together."

"Who are you thinking?"

"Dutch and Onyx. There are a couple of volunteers from the company too."

"Who?"

"Messick and Jacks. Ever heard of them?"

"Ranger Messick started out in counterterrorism. Graduated from Syracuse's INSCT program. Diesel Jacks is a language savant. Speaks twelve at last count. Went to Cornell; almost immediate post-grad recruitment. Both were on Striker's core team."

"You're like a damn computer."

"Want height and weight too?"

"No, thanks."

"You sure about sending Dutch in?"

"He came to me."

"Roger that. What else do you need from me?"

"I need you to look after Alegria. I know you have a lot going on right now, but she won't come here."

"You've asked?"

"No, but my gut tells me she won't."

"Where is she now?"

"She and Dutch are traveling. My understanding is they'll arrive sometime tonight."

"Does she know he's deploying?"

"Negative."

"Shit."

"Sorry, Raze."

"Don't be. I got this."

Instead of getting the SUV, I called my wife. "We have a situation."

—*Ava*—

"What's going on?"

"Can you go somewhere that Aine can't hear you?"

"Sure. Give me a sec." I went into the en-suite bathroom in our room and closed the door. "Okay. I can talk."

"K19 is sending in a team…shit. Ava, you can't say any of this to Aine. Do you promise me you won't?"

I took a deep breath. "I won't, Tabon, I promise."

"Striker and Mantis are MIA."

"Okay."

"Dutch and Onyx are leading a team in, and that means Alegria is going to need our help."

"Tell me what I can do."

"Isn't one of the girls planning to become a PA."

"Pen, and she already is."

"Perfect. I need to think this through, but I'll get back to you in a few. Stay where you are."

"Tabon?"

"Yeah, sweetheart."

"You're sending a team in. That means Striker is still alive, right?"

"I honestly don't know."

I looked in the mirror and took several deep breaths. What I was about to do would be one of the hardest things I'd ever done. I was going to have to lie to my twin, repeatedly. Some would be out-and-out lies and others would be lies of omission. I just prayed that Aine didn't catch on to either.

—*Razor*—

Alegria wasn't exactly a girly-girl, which meant convincing her to hang out with Ava's best friends wasn't going to be an easy sell. But she was part of the K19 team, and as such, we had to give her the support she needed, even if she didn't want it.

"How many bedrooms in the guest house?" I asked Gunner.

"Three. Why?"

"Who's staying in it?"

"For Christ's sake—*why?*"

I pulled Gunner outside. "There's a team goin' in after Striker and Mantis. Dutch is on it. He and Alegria are on their way here, and he's shipping out tonight."

Gunner scrubbed his face with his hand. "Let me think what my mother said. I'm pretty sure she had Dutch and Alegria penciled in. And Odette."

"Can we move your sister?"

"Nice, Raze. Why? Princess Alegria needs her privacy?"

"Penelope and Tara are here."

"What did you bring them in for, moral support?"

I looked out at the bay.

"You did, didn't you?"

"Aine is my sister-in-law, and she's f'ing miserable, and it's Christmas."

Gunner put his hands on his hips. "I don't even recognize us anymore."

"Me either."

"Okay. Let me see where we can stick my sister."

"Wait. Did you say it had three bedrooms?"

"Now what?"

"Well, Aine."

"One of the bedrooms has two twin beds in it. Which means Odette can stay in the main house in the room Aine was slated for."

"See? That wasn't so bad."

Gunner walked away, muttering, but I didn't care. My mission was accomplished, at least the first part of it.

12

Aine and Striker

—*Aine*—

As happy as I was to see Pen and Tara, the horrible feeling of missing Griffin stayed firmly planted in the middle of my chest. What was supposed to be the beginning of our relationship, had ended on Thanksgiving when he suddenly had to leave and couldn't tell me where he was going.

That was the last time I'd seen him or heard his voice—outside of my dreams.

Every time I closed my eyes, I could see him. His blond hair was darker, and his eyes were a lighter shade of blue than mine were. Until he brought up our age difference, I hadn't given it a second thought. His features were timeless, almost prince-like. It wasn't just that his name sounded regal, like Ava had said; he looked it.

While he wasn't as big muscle-wise as Gunner, I could attest that he was rock solid. With eight-pack abs, buff arms, and carved legs, he looked more like the special forces guy he was than a Prince Charming.

It was his vulnerability that had attracted me to him in the first place. When he'd walked down to the beach where my sister was marrying his teammate, he looked uncomfortable, unsure of himself. After spending time with Razor, I found the lack of arrogance refreshing.

I'd been more surprised than startled when he boldly approached me and started a conversation. I'd put my hand on my heart because it felt as though it would beat out of my chest from being so close to him.

"I'm sorry. I didn't mean to startle you," he'd said and introduced himself as Striker. Eventually he'd told me his name was actually Griffin Ellis, and the other thing he'd said was that I was beautiful.

When he mentioned being hungry, I led him up to the kitchen, where we'd made peanut butter and jelly sandwiches and spent enough time talking that my mother had come looking for me.

I put my arms around my waist and closed my eyes. "Where are you?" I whispered. "When will you come back to me?"

—Striker—

"Fuck," I spat when I counted the number of Somali pirates holding whom they believed were journalists. They weren't. Not even close. They were two of the best operatives who'd ever worked for the CIA. Both had been part of my team, and I'd die before I'd leave them there to meet the same fate.

Mantis and I were more than one hundred miles outside of Mogadishu, in Dinlave, a village on the Wabi Shebelle River.

The pirates hadn't brought their captives out here where there wouldn't be any means to communicate with the rest of the world; it was just where they'd run out of money.

Unfortunately, they weren't strangers to the region, which meant their numbers had doubled.

I rolled to my back and looked up at the star-filled night sky. I closed my eyes and thought of Aine, like I did most every time I began to wonder what the hell I was doing.

With no way to summon reinforcements, and a lack of a trail for anyone to find us, Mantis and I had two options. We could leave, and likely never be able to locate the men again, or we could stay and craft a plan to rescue them.

"What day is it?" I asked Mantis.

"The twenty-first of December."

Which meant tomorrow would be thirty days since I'd last seen the woman who graced my dreams as much as haunted them.

"I have an idea," said Mantis.

"Yeah? Is it a good one?"

"I think it is."

I sat up. "Let's hear it."

—*Aine*—

My face hurt from the fake smile I'd plastered on it.

"I love this little house," said Tara, rummaging around in the kitchen. "The main house is nice, but this is…cozy."

I turned around and rolled my eyes. I loved Tara, but cozy had never been her style. I thought the woman was going to have a panic attack when Pen volunteered the two of them to share the bedroom with twin beds.

"It's only fair. We're crashing the party, so to speak."

We'd all agreed that Alegria should take the master bedroom when she arrived since she was still recovering from surgery.

"The woman was shot," Pen said to Tara when she protested. "When you get shot, you can take the big bedroom."

The memory the three of us shared of being kidnapped and held hostage, sat far too close to the surface, although we never spoke of it. I wondered if Alegria had been part of the team that rescued us. Probably, which meant we should thank her, but I doubted any of us would bring it up—especially not Alegria herself.

"What time is dinner?" Tara asked.

I checked my phone. "Twenty minutes."

"Should we walk over?"

"Sure," I murmured, stealing a quick glance of the only photo I had of Griffin and then wishing I hadn't. It only made the pain in my chest hurt worse.

"What is all that?" Pen asked, pointing to the pile of packages from our afternoon shopping spree.

"Most of it belongs to Zary. We took her shopping today so she could get Christmas gifts. She's never done it before."

"Given Christmas gifts or gone shopping?" asked Tara with a smirk.

"Celebrated Christmas."

I told them Zary's story, leaving out the part about her being the one who'd tracked Tara, Pen, and me to Washington where we were being held hostage by Armenians who wanted to lure my father out of hiding. I also left out the part about Zary being our half-sister—until Tara opened her big mouth again.

"She seems weird."

"Tara," admonished Pen.

"What? She's—"

"She's my sister, and she isn't the slightest bit weird. She's led a life none of us can imagine the horrors of, let alone ever be as badass as she is."

"Wait. What?" said Pen. "She's your sister?"

"That's right, and the night we were rescued, she was kidnapped in our place." That wasn't exactly accurate, but it was close enough for me to make my point.

"Sorry. Didn't mean to touch on a nerve."

In that moment, I hated Tara. She wasn't apologizing for what she said about Zary; she was being sarcastic—one of her worst habits.

Every condescending thing that had ever come out of her mouth roared to the surface of my memory. "You're such a bitch," I said, storming out of the guest house's front door. It wasn't like me; Ava was usually the one to call people out on their shit. In the world of good twin, bad twin, I soothed hurt feelings and helped mend fences.

It was cold outside, and in my haste, I hadn't grabbed a jacket. I picked up my pace and was almost to the main house's back door when I heard voices.

"No leads at all?" I heard Gunner ask.

"None. Which is why the team is going in." That was Razor's voice.

"I know I act like I can't stand Striker, and sometimes he annoys the shit outta me, but he's one of us and I respect him. Those Somali bastards can be worse than ISIS."

"I agree. I respect him too. As far as the Somalis are concerned, they operate without a plan. They kidnap without realizing who they've got and then issue ludicrous ransom demands. Remember a few years ago when a group of them kidnapped that journalist along with an Asian fisherman? They demanded twenty mil each. The fisherman's family couldn't have had more than twenty bucks."

"I remember it well. I was on the rescue team."

"That's right. How did you find them? And before you go into detail, understand that what I'm saying is you should brief Dutch as soon as you can."

"Roger that."

When I heard a door open and close, I crept around to the front of the house and rang the bell.

"Goodness, you're practically frozen," said Gunner's mother when she opened the door and pulled me inside. "What were you doing out there?"

My eyes met Gunner's.

"Eavesdropping," he answered for me.

—Striker—

"I like your plan," I said. "Except I'm staying here. If you can't make contact, keep going until you can, even if it means going as far as Mogadishu."

Mantis shook his head. "I don't want to leave you here."

"We don't have a choice. If the Somalis move, someone needs to be able to track them."

"It isn't necessary to state the obvious, but I have no way to track *you*, Striker."

"We talked about this. I'll leave a trail."

Mantis had been gone two hours when I heard the roar of a low-flying Orion plane. It filled me with as much dread as hope because, as I could've predicted, it sent the Somali pirates into chaotic panic. There was no question they'd be on the move before daylight.

—Aine—

I followed Razor into the upstairs bedroom, feeling like a petulant child.

"Tell me what you heard," he coaxed in a gentle tone.

"Everything."

"What's going on?" asked Ava, joining us.

"Aine overheard Gunner and I talking about Striker's mission." Razor turned to me. "Ask me whatever questions you have, and I'll do my best to answer them."

"Tell her everything, Tabon," Ava pleaded.

"The call that Striker got on Thanksgiving was to let him know two of his former team members have been kidnapped by Somali pirates. Striker volunteered to go in after them. Originally, Mantis was only tasked with transportation, but once he knew what the mission was, he volunteered to go in as well."

I nodded.

"It's been over a week without contact, so Doc called earlier about putting a team together to go in and look for them. Dutch Miller had already volunteered. Once he drops Alegria off here, he and Onyx will meet up with two other CIA operatives. The four of them will leave for Mogadishu shortly thereafter."

"Do the pirates have Griffin?"

Razor scrubbed his face with his hand. "We don't know."

"If you don't mind, I'd like to be alone for a few minutes."

"Of course." Razor left the room, but Ava didn't.

"I'm so sorry this is happening, Aine, but Tabon believes they'll be able to find Striker and Mantis."

"You knew already?"

Ava nodded. "Not for very long, though. Tabon needed my help with Alegria. Her recovery is slow, and with Dutch deploying, she needs support from some-where—somebody—else. He believes she'll resist."

"What kind of help?"

"Dutch has been forcing her to do her physical therapy, but he's worried that without his insistence, she'll give up."

"Pen is a physicians' assistant."

Ava nodded. "You're catching on."

"It wasn't a coincidence that they showed up."

"No, but helping Alegria wasn't the original intent."

"What was?"

"Tabon asked them to come because he thought it might help cheer you up."

I wasn't sure how to feel about that. Should I be pissed at him or grateful? "Did you know?"

Ava shook her head. "No clue. I was as surprised as you were."

"Razor is a good man."

"The best," agreed Ava. "So is Striker."

"What can I do to help with Alegria?"

"What you always do, Aine. Be her friend and let her know you empathize in a way no one else can right now."

—Striker—

I stayed low, doing my best to see whether the pirates were preparing to move, and if so, how many of them would leave the encampment. I didn't see signs of mobilization, though, which puzzled me.

The biggest issue I had right now was that Mantis had taken our only vehicle. If the Somalis did move, I'd have to steal one of theirs in order to follow them.

I prayed my teammate had been successful in contacting Doc or someone else from K19 to give them the Somalians' coordinates. If the kidnappers moved, I'd have to as well. I wouldn't be able to wait for Mantis to return.

13

Mantis, Alegria, and Dutch

—Dutch—

For the last three weeks, my relationship with Alegria had been strained to the point of snapping. We hardly spoke except to argue, and the limitations she had to accept as part of her recovery made her irritable.

I knew that wasn't the only thing contributing to her overall cantankerous mood; no one had heard from Mantis in over a week. Neither she nor I had heard from him since he walked out of Razor's house on Thanksgiving.

"We're cleared to go in," Doc said when I answered his call.

"I want to be the lead."

"Done. With Alegria grounded, Onyx is our only option to fly your team to Africa. I'll have to contract a co-pilot."

"Let me talk to him and see if he has anyone he'd recommend," I offered.

"I'd appreciate it."

"Hey, Doc, would you mind keeping this between us until I have time to brief Alegria."

"Say no more."

"Thanks."

I had to figure out a way to tell Alegria not just about the mission, but who I was going in to extract.

I went into the kitchen to grab something to eat, regretting that my time at the house I was rarely at, was coming to such an abrupt end after such a short visit.

I'd purchased and renovated it back when I was stationed at Langley. Originally, I'd intended to flip it, but once I finished the updates, I decided not to.

It had always been easy to rent, given its close proximity to the base. Luckily, the last tenant had PCS'd right before Thanksgiving, and I hadn't relisted it.

When we were getting ready to leave Cambria after Thanksgiving, I asked Alegria what she thought about going to Newport News with me when she was cleared for travel.

"If I could get home, I wouldn't be such a burden to you."

"Meaning where? New York?" As far as I knew, she hadn't set foot in the apartment her parents had purchased for her in more than a year, maybe longer.

"Marseille," she'd responded as though I were an idiot.

"Manon…we need to talk," I said when she walked into the kitchen.

That got her attention. I rarely called her by anything but her Air Force pilot call sign.

"About?"

"There's a mission…"

Her eyes met mine, and whatever anger she'd been feeling moments ago seemed to morph into worry. "What is it?"

—Mantis—

I was almost to Mogadishu when I saw the roadblock. Two decrepit-looking pickup trucks, both mounted with heavy, ancient artillery, were waiting.

A dozen men jumped off of each and swarmed my Jeep, firing into the air all around me. They pulled me out, hit me over the head, and dragged me to one of their vehicles. There was blood seeping from a gash in my scalp, which my captors chose to ignore.

I spoke enough Arabic to understand they were taking me north and inland to Cadaado, the opposite direction of Mogadishu and Dinlave, where Striker was waiting.

Near sundown we arrived at our destination. Even after the sun had set, it was still at least one hundred degrees.

I was blindfolded and led to a foam mattress. I could hear several Somalis yelling and what sounded like other hostages being beaten.

Merry Christmas, I thought to myself. *Welcome to hell.*

—Alegria—

Before he'd even told me about the mission, I had a sick feeling in the pit of my stomach. At first I thought it was not knowing whether Mantis would show up for Christmas like he had for Thanksgiving. This felt worse, though, as if something was terribly wrong.

"When do you leave?" I asked, knowing it had to be soon.

"Tonight. Look, I know it's almost Christmas, and I'm sorry—"

I held up my hand. "Don't be. I understand."

"I wasn't sure you would."

"What do you mean?"

"If Mantis had sprung something like this on you…"

I rested my hand on his arm. "This is different. If the situations were reversed and he was telling me he had to go in and extract you, I would understand in the same way I do now."

Dutch reached out and stroked my cheek. "We'll leave at sixteen hundred."

I nodded and moved closer to him, wishing we hadn't spent the last three weeks arguing as much as we had.

"I'm worried about you," he said, kissing each of my eyelids, my cheeks, and then my lips. "You're very pale."

I shook my head. "It's nothing. Probably withdrawals from the pain meds messing with me."

"The doctor told you it was too soon to stop taking them."

I wrapped my arms around his waist and rested my head on his chest. It felt so good to just relax into his comfort.

"Are you sure you want this?" he murmured before he brought his lips to mine a second time.

I backed away, took his hand, and led him into the bedroom.

Once there, I pulled my sweater over my head, and then pushed my wool skirt down until it slid from my hips to the floor. Dutch's eyes traveled the length of my body as I stood before him in nothing but my bra and panties.

"Make love to me, Dutch." I held my hand out to him and sat on the bed.

In seconds he was on me, as though he was hurrying to get me naked before he changed his mind. His fingers released the clasp on my bra, and he pulled it from me.

"Lie down," he said, taking my panties in both hands and sliding them down my legs.

"Please touch me, Dutch," I begged as he stood above me, studying my body.

I watched as he undressed, walked to the bedside table, opened the drawer, and pulled out a foil packet. He rolled on the condom and came to rest between my legs. "Do you know how much I love you?"

I nodded, but I couldn't look him in the eye.

"Manon…"

"I'm sorry…I can't…" I cried, tears running down my cheeks.

Dutch got off the bed and went into the bathroom. He came back out seconds later, grabbed his clothes, and stalked from the bedroom.

"Get dressed. We'll leave as soon as you're ready," I heard him say.

—Dutch—

I dressed as I went, storming out the back door, into the garage, and over to the punching bag that hung from the rafters. I slammed my fists into it over and over again, cursing my stupidity.

She wasn't mine. She never really had been. Alegria used me to ease the pain of losing Mantis. Why couldn't I accept that as the truth? Why did I talk myself out of it only to have the reality hit me in the face again? *Because I loved her.* As much of an idiot as that made me, I'd loved her since the day we met.

She was everything I'd ever wanted in a woman. She was beautiful, brash, and smart as hell. She had a wicked sense of humor, and for a while, I'd believed I had as much of a shot at getting her to date me as Mantis had. Even then, I'd been lying to myself.

Our drive to Annapolis was silent. When I turned on music, Alegria abruptly turned it off and sat with her arms crossed. She refused to look at or speak to me, although I had nothing to say to her either.

—Mantis—

Sometime during the night, one of the Somalis woke me and handed me a piece of stale bread, a can of tuna, and a bottle of water. After I ate, the same man led me to a hole in the ground where he motioned for me to urinate. After I had, the man led me back to the mattress, chained my legs together first, and then my hands.

The next morning, they dragged me out into the sunlight and tossed me in the back of a pickup truck along with two other men chained like I was. We were blindfolded and gagged before the truck jerked into gear.

When it stopped more than an hour later, my blindfold was removed, and I saw we'd been brought to a different dwelling. The sun was blazing, and without having had water since the night before, I felt faint from dehydration.

When one of the other captives fell on the way inside the house, the man leading him kicked him repeatedly before dragging him the rest of the way in.

I did everything I could to stay on my feet, hoping that once we were inside, we'd be given something to drink, at least. If I didn't hydrate soon, I'd likely become delirious.

"What your name?" one of the younger-looking Somalis asked me.

"Jim," I said, reciting the name on the fake identification I had on me.

"You okay, Jim?" the kid asked.

"No. I need water."

The Somali left, but returned moments later with two bottles.

"I unchain you, Jim. You no try to escape," he told me.

I nodded, grateful for the drink.

"You rich, Jim?"

"Not at all."

"They asking lot of money for you."

"They won't get it. I have no money."

"No lie, Jim," the kid said, smiling an almost toothless grin and leaving me with my hands unshackled.

—Dutch—

I parked the car in the driveway of Gunner's mother's house and walked around to open the passenger door. Alegria got out and started walking toward the house.

"Aren't you coming inside?" she asked when I didn't move from where I stood.

"Just to bring your bag in."

She walked back over to me. "Be safe," she said, reaching up to touch my face with shaking hands, tears spilling down her cheeks.

"Is that for me or him?" I asked, hearing the edge in my own voice.

"Both of you."

I pulled her to me and held her close. "I love you so much," I murmured, wishing she would say it back, but knowing it would be the worst possible time for her to.

14

—Gunner—

As we sat in the glow of the Christmas tree, I thought about how different my life was not just from the year before, but than I ever imagined it would be.

Zary was snuggled next to me, her breathing so even that I guessed she'd fallen asleep. I tightened my arm around her, loving the feel of her body against mine.

"Thank you for taking Losha to the island last night," she murmured.

"You're welcome." Zary and I hadn't talked about the fact Losha *wasn't* alone, as she'd predicted. Somehow I sensed it wasn't something she was ready to discuss, and that didn't bother me. I wasn't sure I'd ever be ready for that conversation. The less I knew about her friend, the better.

"And thank you for today," she murmured. "My mother wanted nothing else for Christmas. You and Razor gave her the perfect gift."

***

When Topor contacted Svetlana with yet another excuse as to why he couldn't make it for Christmas, I was prepared. I'd installed software on Zary's mother's phone, and within seconds of the call, I knew his exact location.

I didn't call the man until we stood outside the door of his motel room.

"We're here to deliver you to your sister as a Christmas gift," I said when he answered the call he believed was from Svetlana.

Rauf "Topor" Evasov opened the door slowly. "Are you sure you're not here to kill me?"

A few short weeks ago, I would've been eager to put a bullet in the man who stood in front of me, but after hearing Zary's account of the way Topor had cared for her mother all those years, and given the fact that he'd saved the life of the woman I loved, I'd developed a soft spot for him.

"We have one rule," said Razor. "We won't kill anyone on Christmas Eve or Christmas Day. After that, all bets are off." He smiled and held out his hand. "Welcome to the family," he said when Topor shook it.

I had to admit the man looked like shit. I wouldn't ask now, but before we delivered him back to the seedy motel he was staying in—if we brought him back here at all—I'd find out who the man was afraid would find him. If it was protection he needed, it would be easy to arrange. One call to the company, and Rauf Evasov would never have to worry for his life again.

I hadn't told Zary or her mother where Razor and I were going, only that we'd be back soon. I wondered if Svetlana had even noticed her phone, which I now held in my hand, was missing.

"We're back," I yelled when we came in the front door. "Where is everyone?"

"In here," my mother hollered from the kitchen.

"This way, Topor."

"Please, Rauf."

"You got it."

Both Zary and her mother were in the kitchen when Razor, Rauf, and I walked in, and the look on both their faces melted my already-thawed heart.

—Zary—

"Tell me about Christmas," I murmured.

"Past or present?"

"Both."

"As you know, we moved around a lot when I was a kid. My parents always made sure that we had as traditional a Christmas as possible. If my dad was stationed in the States, we'd go to my grandparents' house. If not, my mom would pull out all the stops and decorate the hell out of wherever we were living." Gunner looked around the room we were sitting in. "Kind of like she did here."

"I like it."

"I do too, to be honest."

"Which grandparents did you visit?"

"Both. My father's parents lived here, in what is now the guest house. My mother's parents lived in DC, so only about forty-five minutes from here."

"Your mother's father was the French ambassador."

"That's right. Did she tell you, or did you already know?"

"She did. I asked her to tell me about Christmas too. It was lovely to hear about *Père Noël.*"

"Ah, so you understand why the shoes sitting by the fireplace are filled with carrots and cookies."

"For *Père Noël's* donkey."

"Do you know the donkey's name?"

"I do." I clapped my hands "It's *Gui,* which means mistletoe."

"That's right. Every year up until I turned eleven or twelve, I'd beg my parents to get us a donkey that we could name Gui. At some point, Odette convinced me we'd have better luck asking for a dog."

"And?"

"We never got the dog." Gunner laughed. "I haven't thought about that for years."

"Poor Gunner," I teased. "You never got your Christmas wish."

"Yes, I did," he said, kissing me. "You are all I ever really wished for. You're more. There's only one more thing I want this year."

"What?" I asked, sitting forward.

Gunner slid off the sofa and got down on one knee. "I love you in this lifetime just like I did in all the past lifetimes that I know we've spent together. I'll never stop loving you, Zary. Not even when I take my last breath, because I know that in my next life, you'll be by my side again." He slid his hand into his pocket and pulled out a ring. "Marry me, Rocket Girl."

"Oh, Gunner," I cried, sliding off the sofa like he had and throwing my arms around his neck.

"Is that a yes?"

"It's a thousand lifetimes of yes," I said, brushing my lips against his.

"Let's see if this fits." He slid the ring on my finger. "Perfect," he murmured.

"It's so beautiful," I said, gazing at the oval diamond surrounded by rubies.

"There's something I want to tell you, my sweet, wonderful, soon-to-be wife."

My eyes met his.

"I'd like us to be married on the Fourth of July."

I nodded. "Okay…"

"Do you want to know why?"

"Sure."

"It's your birthday."

"What?" I whispered.

"I asked your mother."

"I didn't know."

Gunner helped me back onto the sofa and pulled me close to him. "I'm sorry I didn't tell you right away, but I wanted to surprise you." He ran his finger over the rubies on my ring. "These are your birthstone."

I couldn't stop crying, but Gunner just smiled at me between kisses.

Most of my life, I'd believed whatever year it was would be my last. People in my line of work didn't live to be very old, especially women.

This year was so different. Not only was I with Gunner, my only dream come true, but by next Christmas, we'd have a baby. My mother was sleeping safely and soundly upstairs, and even my uncle was here.

"July fourth," I whispered.

"Is that okay with you?"

"I love it, Gunner."

We heard someone coming down the stairs and turned to see Ava followed by Razor.

"Sorry to interrupt," she said, rubbing her belly. "I needed a snack."

I squeezed Gunner's hand and leapt off the sofa. "Look," I squealed. "Gunner and I are getting married."

"Oh my gosh. Let me see," Ava cried, looking at the ring. "It's so beautiful."

"We're getting married on July fourth," I announced. "And, it's my birthday."

—Gunner—

"Congratulations, man," said Razor, clapping me on the back. "You did good."

"Look at her," I murmured.

Razor smiled. "I am," he murmured, but I could see he wasn't looking at Zary; he was looking at Ava. "I never dreamed…" my friend said.

"Me either." I wiped at the tear forming at the edge of my eye.

"We're gonna be brothers," said Razor.

"Huh?"

"Brothers-in-law. Same thing, right?"

"We've always been brothers, Raze."

"I feel the same way."

"Where'd they go?" I asked, looking for Zary and Ava.

"My guess is kitchen."

—Zary—

"I crave pancakes more than anything else. Oh, and bacon. Especially late at night," said Ava.

"I don't know if I crave anything. Is that weird?"

"I have no idea, but you probably do without even realizing it."

"You crave bananas," said Gunner, walking up and putting his arm around my shoulders.

"That's true."

"And pierogies with sauerkraut."

I laughed. "You're right. Wow." I turned to Ava. "I could eat pierogies every day."

"Same with pancakes for me."

"I thought I heard somebody in my kitchen," said Madeline, padding out of the bedroom.

"Sorry, Ma, did we wake you?"

"No. We were just talking," she answered, pointing to my mother, who walked out behind her.

"Merry Christmas!" my mother shouted, and everyone laughed.

"Look, Mama," I said, walking up to her and Madeline. *"On poprosil menya vyyti za nego zamuzh."*

"Rubies," my mother whispered.

"Yes," I nodded.

"Four iyulya."

"What is she saying?" Madeline asked.

"Zary's birthday is July fourth," Ava whispered.

When my mother let me go, I hugged Gunner's mother.

"I'm so happy for you," she cried, and then looked at Gunner. "And I'm so proud of you."

"What's going on?" asked Odette, coming in from the front of the house. "I can hear you all the way upstairs."

"Your brother proposed." Madeline pulled me by the hand over to where Odette was standing.

"Wow." She studied the ring. "You did good."

"That's what I said," Razor added.

"So, why are we in the kitchen?" Madeline asked.

"Pancakes," chirped Ava.

"And pierogies," I added.

"I think I can manage both." Madeline winked, opening the refrigerator and pulling out a bowl. "Your mother made these this morning," she said, showing me the pierogies.

I hugged my mom. *"Spasibo."*

My mother kissed my cheek. "Merry Christmas!" she said again.

Gunner put his arm around my waist and I felt a sense of peace I never dreamed possible.

"This is the best Christmas ever," he whispered.

"I agree." I leaned my body into his.

15

Ava and Razor

—*Ava*—

"I feel like I should go get Aine," I whispered.

"I'll go get her if you want me to," Tabon offered.

"Pen and Tara would probably come with her."

"Are you talking yourself in or out of this?"

I shrugged. "I'm not sure what to say or not say to her. I don't want her to feel left out of something like this, but I don't want to make her sad either."

Tabon leaned over and kissed the side of my face.

"You haven't heard anything?"

He shook his head. "I'm sorry."

"Hey, look, you two," said Odette. "You're standing under the mistletoe."

I looked up. "We are."

Tabon kissed me and everyone clapped.

"When we were kids, Gunner and I *begged* our parents to get us a dog for Christmas."

"I was telling Zary about that a few minutes ago. We wanted to name him *Gui*—"

"French for mistletoe," interrupted Odette.

"That's so sweet," I said, looking at Tabon.

"You want a dog, baby? We can do that."

"Does he say yes no matter what you want?" Odette asked.

I smiled. "Yeah. Pretty much."

"That's what I want for Christmas."

"What's that, sweetheart?" Madeline asked.

"A man who will give me whatever I want."

"Oh, Odette."

"Tired?" Tabon asked when I finished eating a stack of pancakes.

"Yeah. I should clean up, though."

"Don't be silly," said Madeline. "I'm almost finished with the dishes. Go up to bed."

"Thank you," I said, kissing her cheek.

"We should head up too." Gunner stood and pulled Zary's chair out for her.

She looked as tired as I felt.

"I used to have to tell the kids not to even think about getting out of bed before eight on Christmas morning. When they were teenagers, Marchand and I would wake them up at eleven."

"We'll see you somewhere in between the two," said Gunner, kissing his mother's cheek. "Goodnight, Ma."

—Razor—

"Can we really get a dog?" Ava asked once we were in bed.

"Of course."

"You're so agreeable."

"That's because I'm happier than I've ever been in my life." I turned to my side and caressed Ava's face. "I mean that."

"I am too, Tabon. I never dreamed…"

"Gunner and I said the same thing earlier."

"I hope…"

"What? Do you have a Christmas wish you haven't shared with me?"

Ava nodded. "I know it's impossible, but I wish Striker could be here tomorrow."

"Me too." I wouldn't admit it to anyone, especially on Christmas, but there was no trace of either Striker or Mantis anywhere in Somalia.

"You're worried," she said, looking into my eyes.

"More than I want you to know."

Ava's eyes filled with tears.

"See," I said, brushing them away. "This is why I didn't want to say anything. I didn't want to upset you more."

"Why did Striker have to take this assignment? And before you answer, I know it isn't that simple."

"Even less simple, given he mentored the two men who were kidnapped."

"He didn't have a choice," she murmured.

"No, he didn't. Just like I didn't have a choice when you were in danger."

"Can we talk about something else?"

"Of course."

"What kind of dog would we get, you know, if we got one?"

"I'd prefer to rescue one from a shelter."

"I like that idea very much." Ava rested her head on my chest. "Merry Christmas, Tabon."

"Merry Christmas, Avarie."

—Ava—

I opened my eyes and sat up. Tabon wasn't in bed with me. I got up, looked out the window, and saw it'd snowed the night before. The sun was shining, and everything looked as though it were covered in a blanket of diamonds.

Aine poked her head in the door. "Hey, sleepyhead. Are you ever gonna get up?"

"I'm up. What time is it?"

"A little after ten."

"Why didn't someone wake me earlier?"

"We thought it would be a good idea to let the two preggos sleep. Zary isn't awake yet either."

"In that case, come sit for a minute."

"Ava…"

"You can pretend all you want with everyone else, but you have to be honest with me. How are you holding up?"

"Honestly, I'm okay."

"What changed?"

"I talked to Alegria."

"And?"

"She told me that Griffin and Mantis are the best of the best. Just because they're out of contact, doesn't necessarily mean anything is wrong. It only means that they don't think it's safe to make contact."

"Did she say anything else?"

"So much. We talked almost all night."

I folded my arms. "Are you going to make me keep asking what you talked about?"

"She told me about a few of their missions, without divulging any *classified* information, of course."

"And?"

"There have been so many. She told me I'd get used to it. I'd always worry, but the more missions Griffin came back from safely, the more I'd trust how good he is at what he does."

"She's not worried about Mantis?"

"The way she put it, is that she's worried, but she knows the team is made up of professionals who have been trained to do this kind of work."

I wondered how much of what Aine was telling me she believed, and how much was my sister putting on a brave face.

"Did you hear about Gunner and Zary?" I asked, changing the subject.

"No. What happened?"

"They got engaged last night. Wait until you see her ring. It's gorgeous."

"Come on," said Aine, pulling me up from where she'd sat on the bed. "Let's go wake her up."

—Razor—

"What's going on?" Gunner asked me.

"With what?"

"Don't pull that with me. You're acting…sneaky."

I laughed out loud. "Oh, yeah? I'm sneaky? Good thing I got into the line of work I did."

"You know damn well what I mean. You're up to something."

I shrugged. "You're imagining things."

"The hell I am," Gunner grumbled, walking away.

I breathed a very temporary sigh of relief. If Ava and Zary didn't get up soon, the surprise I had planned would be ruined.

I bounded up the stairs two at a time, but when I got to the bedroom Ava and I had slept in, it was empty. Seconds later, I heard her voice down the hallway.

"Good morning," I said, walking into the room where she was talking to Zary and Aine. "The three of you do realize it's Christmas, right?"

"Aine said you were letting us sleep in."

"And we were, but how much longer do you think we can hold off Sierra and Savannah?"

"I forgot about them," Ava gasped, covering her mouth with her hand. "Those poor little girls. Why didn't you wake us up?"

"No need to get violent," I said when she swatted me. I looked over at Zary, who had the sheet pulled up to her neck.

"Uh, I think we should give your sister some privacy." I took Ava and Aine by the hand and pulled them toward the door.

"Hurry up," Ava hollered back at Zary.

"I'll be right down after I dress," she hollered back.

Ava wrenched her hand from mine. "Give me a sec," she said and walked back to the bedroom door. "It's Christmas; you're supposed to stay in your pajamas."

When Zary didn't answer, Ava walked back over to me. "Okay, Mr. Pushy, let's hurry up and get downstairs."

I nuzzled up against her and pushed her in the direction of our bedroom. "We could take a quick detour."

"No way." She smirked. "We can't hold off Savannah and Sierra any longer."

I left Ava in the kitchen and went to look for Gunner's sister.

"You were a damn good actress last night," I said to Odette, following her out to the garage.

"It's a good thing my dad had heaters installed out here."

—Ava—

"Where did Tabon disappear to?" I asked when Zary came downstairs. "Everyone is here but him, now." I stood to go look for him.

"Odette is missing too," said Madeline.

I heard the front door open, followed by the sound of a small herd of elephants bounding in.

"*Puppies!*" Savannah and Sierra squealed, trying to corral the three little balls of fur.

"Whose are they?" Sierra asked, giggling when the one she caught licked her face.

"That one is yours and Sierra's," Saylor told her daughter.

"And this one is ours." Tabon handed me the puppy he'd scooped up.

"And what about that one?" I asked, pointing to the puppy nuzzling against Zary.

"That one is *Gui*," Odette answered, looking at Gunner.

"Seriously?" he asked.

"Yep," she smiled.

"How could you tell the difference?" I asked. "They all look alike. What kind of dogs are they?"

"Odette and I decided that they'd pick their owners, and they did, and they're mutts. When the shelter told us they had three from the same litter, we scooped them up."

"Hey, Sis?" said Gunner.

"Yeah," answered Odette.

"Would you mind if we called him Mistletoe?"

She laughed. "Call him whatever you want. He's your puppy. I'm just his auntie."

"That means you're an auntie too," I said to Aine as I put the puppy in my sister's arms.

"He's so sweet," she murmured.

"Uh, I think he's a she," said Tabon, lifting the puppy's tail.

"What should we name her?" I asked, scratching the puppy's ears.

"We're naming ours Jingle Bells," shouted the girls, who were rolling around the floor while their dog jumped over them and back again.

"How about Dasher?" suggested Aine when the puppy squirmed out of her arms and raced across the room.

"Perfect," I said, looking at Tabon, who nodded.

"This is the best Christmas ever," said Sierra, hugging her mom.

"I agree," whispered Tabon, kissing my cheek.

"Me too," I whispered back.

16

Aine and Striker

—Striker—

"The boss isn't gonna like this," Onyx said.

"Which boss is that? Because from where I sit, we're all the boss."

"I'll tell Doc you said that when he rips me a new one."

"It's Christmas. He's not going to do any such thing." I looked at my watch. "Can't you drive any faster?"

"I didn't fly all the way back from Africa just to get in a car accident on the damn Maryland Turnpike."

"If you don't hurry up, Christmas is going to be over."

—Aine—

I rested my head on my mother's shoulder.

"I'm proud of you," she said.

"Me? Why?"

"I know how worried you are, but you aren't showing a bit of it to anyone in this room."

"I'm okay—"

She kissed my cheek. "Neither of you girls think I know anything about you, but you're wrong. I admit that I wasn't a very good mother to you, but that doesn't mean I can't tell when you're hurting."

"I'm sorry, Mom."

"What for?"

"That you think that about us."

"How could you not, sweetheart? I'm the first to admit I wasn't there for either of you when I should've been. If you'll let me, I'll spend the rest of my life making it up to you and your sister."

"As long as you're part of our lives, that'll be enough for us, Mom."

"I'm so full," said Ava, rubbing her belly.

"And yet, you'll be eating again in a half hour."

My sister pouted. "That isn't very nice, Aine."

"Tellin' like it is, Sis."

"Where are you going?" Ava asked when I got off the sofa.

"To clean up."

"I'll help."

"No. Stay there. If you get up, Dasher will too, and I don't feel like chasing her all over the house."

"Is that how you're going to be with your niece or nephew?"

"Only if he or she comes out of the womb walking."

I rubbed my neck and went into the kitchen.

"Tired?" my mom asked.

"Yeah. Wait. What happened in here?"

"What do you mean?" Razor's mother asked.

"Ten minutes ago, it was a wreck."

"It was more like thirty minutes ago," said Madeline, putting her arm around Svetlana's shoulders.

"It's called teamwork, darling," said my mother. "Don't you know that moms are the ones who really rule the world?"

"I believe it," I murmured, looking at the spotless counters.

"Oh no," Madeline gasped when she heard the doorbell followed by the raucous of barking puppies. "Who could that be at this hour? It's after nine o'clock."

"Hey, Aine?" I heard my sister call. "I need your help for a minute."

"She's gonna be like this until she has the baby, isn't she?" I said to my mother.

"Longer." She laughed. "Most likely until that baby is off to college."

"Aine?" Ava hollered again.

"Coming, princess," I shouted back.

—Striker—

There was no more beautiful sight in the world than the look on Aine's face when she came out of the kitchen. She smiled and cried—all at once.

"Hi," I said as she ran into my arms.

"Griffin? Oh my God. Are you real?"

"Merry Christmas, sweetheart. I got here as fast as I could."

"How? When? *How?*" she asked, not giving me a chance to answer between her endless stream of kisses.

I glanced at all the eyes around the room focused on us. "If you all wouldn't mind excusing us, I'm sure Onyx will answer whatever questions you have. Right, buddy?" I squeezed my teammate's shoulder as I led Aine out of the room. "Is there somewhere private we can talk?" I asked once we were out of earshot from everyone.

"Come with me." She led me through the house.

"What the hell, how big is this place?" I asked as we went from room to room until we reached the door that led to the enclosed porch.

"Tell me what happened. I was so worried. How did Onyx find you?"

"We have all the time in the world for that, Aine. Right now, I want to hear about you. I missed you so much."

"I missed you too. So much."

I kissed her and pulled her body flush with mine. "All I could think about was how I didn't want you to spend Christmas alone."

"I wasn't. As you could see, there's a houseful of people here."

"I meant without me."

Aine smiled. "I know. I'm so happy to see you."

"I have a condo about an hour from here, would—"

"Yes."

"Yes, you want to go, or yes, you'd mind?"

"Yes, I want to go, as soon as you do."

"How about right now?"

"You don't have to talk to anyone, or…"

"I'm here to see you. I don't give reindeer poop about anyone else."

Aine laughed, and it was such a sweet sound. There was only one sweeter, and I intended to hear it over and over again once we were at my condo and alone.

—Aine—

"Merry Christmas, everyone!" I shouted as Griffin and I stood by the front door and waved.

"I guess you're gonna want these, Striker," said Onyx, handing me a set of keys.

"Thanks, man. Uh, I don't really care right now, but what are you gonna do for a ride?"

"I haven't slept in over thirty-six hours. The only thing I need right now is a flat surface to fall asleep on."

"Come with me," said Madeline. "I have the perfect place for you to get some rest."

"Where are you taking him?" asked Gunner.

"He'll sleep in my room tonight," she told her son. "I'll sleep in the guest house with the girls."

"No, ma'am, I can't do that," I heard Onyx say.

"He can sleep in my room," said Peggy, walking up to Onyx. "I don't know how you did it, but you brought Griffin back to my daughter, and for that, I'll be eternally grateful. I'll be the one who sleeps in the guest house with the girls tonight."

"Should we sneak out now?" Striker asked.

"Let me just say goodnight to my mom. She deserves a hug for saying that to Onyx. He does too, actually."

He put his arm around my shoulder. "You can hug your mom, but I don't want Onyx anywhere near you."

"Why not?"

Griffin made a growling sound. "You're mine."

"Don't be silly. I can thank the man."

I twisted away and walked over to my mom.

"Thanks," I said, hugging her tight.

"I'm happy for you, baby girl."

I felt myself tearing up, and pulled away.

"Thank you," I said to Onyx, stepping forward to hug him.

"Look!" shouted Sierra. "You're under the mistletoe. You're supposed to kiss."

Before I could react, I felt Griffin's hand on my arm. He made the growling sound again. "Get outta here, Onyx," he said before he kissed me.

What I thought would be a chaste one so we could leave quickly, turned into something that foreshadowed the night to come.

"Let's go somewhere we don't have an audience," I murmured.

"I'm with you, sweetheart."

We waved a final goodbye and walked out to the car.

"I can't wait to get you alone," he said, kissing me again when he opened the passenger door.

"I can't wait either."

"My place might be a little chilly, I haven't been home for a while."

"I don't care. You'll keep me warm."

"You got that right."

—Striker—

The hour-long drive to my house felt five times that long. Every few seconds, I'd look over at Aine, whose eyes never wavered from me.

"Do you know how happy I am to be with you?" I asked.

"It can't be half as happy as I am."

I brought her hand to my lips. "I thought about you every minute."

For the first time, she looked away from me.

"Talk to me, Aine. What's on your mind?"

"Nothing." She shook her head.

"No. Come on. You promised you'd talk things out with me."

"It can wait, Griffin."

"You either tell me what's bothering you now, or I'll pull this car over, and we'll park until you do."

"I know I'm not supposed to ask, though."

"You want to know what happened."

Aine nodded.

"I'll tell you now, but once we get to my place, we won't talk about it again. Fair enough?"

"Yes," she murmured.

"It isn't exactly a Christmas story."

"I know that, Griffin."

"The call I got on Thanksgiving was to inform me that two of the men who were part of my core team at the agency had been kidnapped in Somalia." I looked over at Aine, who nodded.

"Go ahead," she murmured.

"The intel indicated that the kidnappers were Somali pirates—who, historically, are unorganized, under-funded, and that's if they're funded at all. By the time Mantis and I got to headquarters, the ransom call had come in."

"To the CIA?"

"Yes, and no. Tackle and Halo were undercover as journalists in Somalia. The 'newspaper' the pirates contacted was actually a direct line to the agency."

"Tackle and Halo?"

"Knox 'Halo' Clarkson and Landry 'Tackle' Sorenson."

"Where are they now?"

"With their families, and don't ask what that cost me."

"What do you mean?"

"Let's just say their current supervisor wanted them to hang around for a briefing, and I disagreed."

"How did you find them?"

I scrubbed my face with my hand. "You need to understand that what I do, isn't always…pretty."

"If you can't tell me, I understand."

I took a deep breath. "Mantis and I tracked the pirates to a remote part of Somalia, but we were seriously outnumbered. Worse, we had no means of communication. We decided that Mantis would go back to Mogadishu to get reinforcements while I continued to stake out the pirates."

***

When the Somalis went in the direction from which we came, I almost shouted out in happiness. If they were returning to Mogadishu, that meant two things. First, that I'd be able to get in touch with someone back home and get backup. The second thing it meant was I'd reconnect with Mantis, who'd probably already called in the cavalry.

It wasn't difficult for me to nab a vehicle. I'd found a lone Somali about to get in one of their decrepit-looking AWD vehicles, hit him over the head with my gun, knocked him out, and pulled him into a grove of trees. I took the man's clothes, changed into them, and fell into their convoy.

No one paid attention to me during the drive in from the desert, and once I got into the city, I immediately signaled for help.

"We were just headed your way," Dutch said when I answered his call. "We picked up your twenty about five minutes ago."

"You got Mantis?" I asked.

"Negative. He's not with you?"

"No, but he's here in Mogadishu. You haven't been able to track him?"

"Again, that's a negative, sir."

I shook my head, willing a good reason for Mantis to be out of range of contact.

"There are six Somalis transporting Halo and Tackle in. Who's with you?"

"Onyx, Ranger, and Diesel, sir."

"Outstanding. This should be a slam dunk." And it would be if Mantis miraculously materialized.

It wasn't long before I noticed my team's tail. As soon as the Somali bastards turned the next corner, they'd ambush them, get Halo and Tackle, and leave the soon-to-be-dead Somalis behind.

***

"Everything went like clockwork," I told Aine. "Until we had to face the fact that Mantis was still MIA. Dutch had a mole in the city, whom he made contact with. After several hours, we were able to confirm that Mantis had, in fact, been kidnapped right outside the city."

"What did you do then?"

"Dutch ordered Onyx to bring me back to the States, and to be honest, with the shape I was in, it was the right call. He, Diesel, and Ranger went on to look for Mantis. With the information they had from the mole, they felt confident it wouldn't take them long."

"Have you heard anything?"

"I haven't." What I wouldn't admit to Aine, or out loud to anyone, was that the team should've found Mantis and reported back to me several hours ago. That they hadn't, filled me with dread. Something had to be wrong.

I'd just pulled into my garage when my phone buzzed. I got it out and looked at the screen.

We found him, the text said.

I would've preferred Dutch had said, "we got him," but I wasn't going to quibble.

Roger that, I answered. *Good job.*

"What's happened?" asked Aine.

"They found him."

"Thank God," she said, breathing out a sigh of relief that should've matched my own, but something still nagged at me.

I checked my phone again, but there was nothing more from Dutch. There were a number of possible explanations why he hadn't sent an update, and many of them were positive. I'd learned a long time ago not to speculate either way until I had hard evidence.

I pushed the situation to the back of my mind, determined to focus on Aine, and the fact that it was still Christmas, and we were together.

"Come on inside, baby," I said, "I'll grab your things."

I set the bag beside the front door and walked through my condo, turning on lights and upping the temperature on the thermostat. I leaned down and arranged a couple of logs in the fireplace, added kindling, and lit the fire.

When I turned around, Aine had a gift bag in her hand.

"I'll be right back." I took the stairs two at a time, knowing exactly where I had the gift I'd thought about giving her the whole time I was in Somalia.

—Aine—

I bit my bottom lip, hoping that Griffin wouldn't think my gift was inappropriate, given we hadn't been seeing each other very long.

When he eyed the bag in my hand and bounded up the stairs, I worried that he felt obligated to give me something too and had gone in search of something he could find at the last minute.

"I brought you a gift. It's just something little," I said when he came back downstairs empty-handed.

"I have something for you too."

"You don't have to. I mean, just because I—"

"I would've given this to you tonight whether you had something for me or not."

I felt the flush creep up my neck and into my cheeks.

Griffin walked closer and put his hand on the back of my neck. "I know we haven't spent as much time together as either of us would've liked, but that doesn't mean I don't feel a connection to you like none I've ever felt before. I know you feel it too."

I nodded. "I do."

Griffin pulled a small box out of his pocket and put it in my hand. "You first," he said.

I lifted the lid. My eyes met Griffin's when I pulled the bracelet out of the box. "It's beautiful."

"It belonged to someone very special to me," he said. "The one person who always loved me unconditionally."

"Who was she, Griffin?"

"My aunt. Her name was Dorothy, and she was my mother's sister. She died a few years ago, but before she did, she gave me this." He ran his finger over the charms, each one adorned with a garnet. "You share a birthday."

"We do?"

Griffin nodded. "January third."

"How did you know?" I asked, immediately realizing the stupidity of the question. "Never mind," I murmured.

"Would you like to wear it?"

"I'd love to." I held out my wrist. Griffin draped the bracelet on it and fastened the clasp.

"It's beautiful."

"Like you."

I felt my face flush again as tears filled my eyes. "It's a family heirloom."

"One I want you to have."

"Will you open yours now?" I asked, handing him the bag.

—Striker—

I reached into the small bag and pulled out what looked like a pocket watch wrapped in tissue. I opened the brass cover and found that, instead of a watch, it was a compass engraved with a message.

If you take me by the hand

Open your heart
I'll help you
Find your way back home.
A.

"Wow," I said, meeting her eyes. "I love it."

"Do you?" she asked, biting her bottom lip.

I ran my fingers over it and leaned forward to kiss her. "I've never loved a gift more."

"Me either," Aine said, running her finger over the garnet charms. "This is the best Christmas I've ever had. Does that sound silly?"

"Not at all," I answered, pulling her close. "It's the best Christmas I've ever had too."

Epilogue

Mantis, Alegria, and Dutch

—Alegria—

I'd spent most of Christmas Eve talking to Aine, reassuring her that the team who had gone in to search for Striker and Mantis, along with the two CIA operatives they'd been tasked with extracting from their Somali pirate kidnappers, were the best of the best. And that Striker and Mantis were too.

I'd all but promised Aine that Striker would come back safe, and was as happy as everyone else when he and Onyx walked in the front door.

Holding my breath, I willed more men to follow, but none did. I waited, listening to Onyx give the condensed version of Striker's rescue, knowing he was leaving out ninety percent of what had actually happened.

"Can we talk?" I asked.

Onyx nodded. "Where?"

"Come with me." I walked out the front door and down the pathway to the guest house.

"Where are Dutch and Mantis?"

"We weren't able to get a fix on Mantis' twenty when we got to Mogadishu, although we had been able to track Striker."

I closed my eyes and took a deep breath. "Go on."

"It wasn't until we were able to intercept Striker that we realized Mantis wasn't with him. Striker was just as surprised that Mantis wasn't with us."

"Please, Onyx. Tell me what happened," I implored, wishing he would just get on with it.

"Dutch has a Somali source who was able to confirm that Mantis had been ambushed on his way into the city. The team agreed that I'd fly Striker, Halo, and Tackle back to the States while Dutch, Ranger, and Diesel went to extract Mantis."

"What have you heard?"

"Nothing yet. Hold on. It's been a while since I've checked." He pulled the phone out and looked at the screen. "They found him."

"They found him?"

"That's what it says."

"Not that they've got him?"

"No, ma'am." Onyx showed me the message.

"Merde."

"I'll follow up."

—Dutch—

Donning my night vision device, I could see Mantis along with two other men, who looked like they were also captives. All were heavily guarded, but that wouldn't deter me or my team from going in and extracting them. We just needed to organize, and then we'd head in.

—Mantis—

My head was throbbing, and I felt nauseous. Whatever I'd last eaten was probably spoiled, or worse—poisoned.

I'd been listening to the Somalis argue about the fact that, so far, no one had responded to their ransom demands.

I doubted it would be long before they heard from either Doc or someone from the CIA, but it would only be to tell them they didn't negotiate with kidnappers and to demand my release.

It was clear that the group who ambushed me was as financially crippled as the one who had taken Tackle and Halo. Nearly everyone in Somalia was in the same situation. Whatever foreign aid came into the country, immediately landed in the hands of corrupt government officials rather than be disbursed to the dying people in their country.

I heard a sound that made my ears prick up. It sounded almost like a birdsong, and would to anyone else who had heard it, but I knew differently.

All hell was about to rain down on this encampment, and not just from anybody; my best friend, Dutch, was here, and I was about to be rescued.

Keep reading for a sneak peek at the next
book in Heather Slade's
K19 Security Solutions Team One Series,
Mantis' Desire

He's a former fighter pilot determined to get her back.
She fell for his friend after he broke her heart. With
MANTIS now back at her side, she's praying for answers.

MANTIS

Even as a pilot, I face battles that take me away, put
my life at risk. When I'm undercover, I sometimes feel
forgotten. Now that I'm back, all that matters is helping Alegria heal. I've loved her since college; I'd do
anything to get her back, to make her happy—even if it
means walking away.

ALEGRIA

I loved him first. He knows that. But he left me. And
when he did, I fell for someone else. Now that he's
back, there's more on the line. Our lives are in danger.
We need a lot more than prayers, we need MANTIS
ready for the fight.

1

Mantis

When I heard the sound that made my ears prick up, I knew all hell would soon rain down on the encampment where I was being held hostage.

The nausea and debilitating headache I'd had only moments ago went away with the rush of adrenaline that flooded my body. Every nerve ending had gone on high alert as I prepared to carry out the procedures I'd been trained to do if I ever found myself in a hostage situation.

My job was to get myself and the other two captives out of the way without alerting our Somali pirate captors of the impending attack.

As with every other mission or op I'd carried out with my lifelong best friend, Thomas "Dutch" Miller, it executed flawlessly.

"Let's go!" Dutch shouted, leading me and the other hostages out of the compound and into waiting vehicles.

I climbed into one SUV with Dutch, and the other four men climbed into the second.

"I owe ya one," I said once we were a safe distance away from the compound.

Dutch laughed. "Oh, yeah? I think I owed you a couple first."

"Let's call it even, then. What's the word on Striker, Tackle, and Halo?"

"Extracted." Dutch scrubbed his face with his hand. "I'm not sure if I should tell you this."

I turned my head and looked at him. "What?"

"They were home in time for Christmas."

I nodded. That wasn't bad news. I wondered why Dutch would think I'd take it as such.

"How are you doin'?"

I rubbed the back of my neck with my hand. "I could use a hot shower, about five gallons of water, and decent food. After that—sleep."

"Tall order, but I think we can manage most of it. Who were the other two prisoners?"

"I don't know. They're not American, I know that much."

"Diesel and Ranger will take care of contacting whichever embassy they should be delivered to."

"How far are we from Mogadishu?"

"Three hours, at least."

"Mind if I get some rest?"

"Of course not."

I reached over the back of the seat and grabbed a blanket. I wadded it up and put it between my head and the passenger side window. As uncomfortable as I was, it was better than where I'd been sleeping the last several days.

About the Author

USA Today and Amazon Top 15 Bestselling Author Heather Slade writes shamelessly sexy, edge-of-your seat romantic suspense.

She gave herself the gift of writing a book for her own birthday one year. Forty-plus books later (and counting), she's having the time of her life.

The women Slade writes are self-confident, strong, with wills of their own, and hearts as big as the Colorado sky. The men are sublimely sexy, seductive alphas who rise to the challenge of capturing the sweet soul of a woman whose heart they'll hold in the palm of their hand forever. Add in a couple of neck-snapping twists and turns, a page-turning mystery, and a swoon-worthy HEA, and you'll be holding one of her books in your hands.

She loves to hear from my readers. You can contact her at heather@heatherslade.com

To keep up with her latest news and releases, please visit her website at www.heatherslade.com to sign up for her newsletter.

MORE FROM AUTHOR HEATHER SLADE

BUTLER RANCH
Kade's Worth
Brodie's Promise
Maddox's Truce
Naughton's Secret
Mercer's Vow
Kade's Return
Butler Ranch Christmas

WICKED WINEMAKERS
FIRST LABEL
Brix's Bid
Ridge's Release
Press' Passion
Zin's Sins
Tryst's Temptation

WICKED WINEMAKERS
SECOND LABEL
Beau's Beloved
Coming Soon:
Cru's Crush
Bones' Bliss
Snapper's Seduction
Kick's Kiss

ROARING FORK RANCH
Coming Soon:
Roaring Fork Wrangler
Roaring Fork Roughstock
Roaring Fork Rockstar
Roaring Fork Rooker
Roaring Fork Bridger

THE ROYAL AGENTS
OF MI6
Make Me Shiver
Drive Me Wilder
Feel My Pinch
Chase My Shadow
Find My Angel

K19 SECURITY
SOLUTIONS TEAM ONE
Razor's Edge
Gunner's Redemption
Mistletoe's Magic
Mantis' Desire
Dutch's Salvation

K19 SECURITY
SOLUTIONS TEAM TWO
Striker's Choice
Monk's Fire
Halo's Oath
Tackle's Honor
Onyx's Awakening

K19 SHADOW OPERATIONS
TEAM ONE
Code Name: Ranger
Code Name: Diesel
Code Name: Wasp
Code Name: Cowboy
Code Name: Mayhem

K19 ALLIED INTELLIGENCE
TEAM ONE
Code Name: Ares
Code Name: Cayman
Code Name: Poseidon
Code Name: Zeppelin
Code Name: Magnet

K19 ALLIED INTELLIGENCE
TEAM TWO
Coming Soon:
Code Name: Puck
Code Name: Michelangelo
Code Name: Typhon
Code Name: Hornet
Code Name: Reaper

PROTECTORS
UNDERCOVER
Undercover Agent
Undercover Emissary
Coming Soon:
Undercover Savior
Undercover Infidel
Undercover Assassin

THE INVINCIBLES
TEAM ONE
Decked
Edged
Grinded
Riled
Smoked

THE INVINCIBLES
TEAM TWO
Bucked
Irished
Sainted
Hammered
Ripped

THE UNSTOPPABLES
TEAM ONE
Furied
Merried

COWBOYS OF
CRESTED BUTTE
A Cowboy Falls
A Cowboy's Dance
A Cowboy's Kiss
A Cowboy Stays
A Cowboy Wins